FMK

MORGAN'S MERCENARIES
IV
MAVERICK HEARTS

**"Lindsay McKenna continues to leave her
distinctive mark on the romance genre
with...timeless tales about the healing
power of love."**
—*Affaire de Coeur*

"I want to kiss you, Paige."

Shivering out of need, Paige barely nodded her
head.

"Good," Thane said roughly as he leaned over, his
eyes closing.

Paige soaked up his strong, cherishing mouth
as it captured hers firmly. She felt the controlled
power of Thane, the way he framed her face
with his large, scarred hands, the roughness of his
skin against her own. How badly she had longed to
touch him, to tell him of the love she had always
held for him—the love he could never know about.

Breaking the kiss, Thane gave her an unsteady
smile. "If I don't stop now, sweetheart, I won't stop
at all...."

"I know," Paige said. Yet, as she drowned in his
burning green gaze, she felt helpless to deny him
anything....

Dear Reader,

As the air begins to chill outside, curl up under a warm blanket with a mug of hot chocolate and these six fabulous Special Edition novels.…

First up is bestselling author Lindsay McKenna's *A Man Alone,* part of her compelling and highly emotional MORGAN'S MERCENARIES: MAVERICK HEARTS series. Meet Captain Thane Hamilton, a wounded Marine who'd closed off his heart long ago, and Paige Black, a woman whose tender loving care may be just what the doctor ordered.

Two new miniseries are launching this month and you're not going to want to miss either one! Look for *The Rancher Next Door,* the first of rising star Susan Mallery's brand-new miniseries, LONE STAR CANYON. Not even a long-standing family feud can prevent love from happening! Also, veteran author Penny Richards pens a juicy and scandalous love story with *Sophie's Scandal,* the first of her wonderful new trilogy— RUMOR HAS IT… that two high school sweethearts are about to recapture the love they once shared.…

Next, Jennifer Mikels delivers a wonderfully heartwarming romance between a runaway heiress and a local sheriff with *The Bridal Quest,* the second book in the HERE COME THE BRIDES series. And Diana Whitney brings back her popular STORK EXPRESS series. Could a *Baby of Convenience* be just the thing to bring two unlikely people together?

And last, but not least, please welcome newcomer Tori Carrington to the line. *Just Eight Months Old…* and she'd stolen the hearts of two independent bounty hunters—who just might make the perfect family!

Enjoy these delightful tales, and come back next month for more emotional stories about life, love and family!

Best,
Karen Taylor Richman
Senior Editor

Please address questions and book requests to:
Silhouette Reader Service
U.S.: 3010 Walden Ave., P.O. Box 1325, Buffalo, NY 14269
Canadian: P.O. Box 609, Fort Erie, Ont. L2A 5X3

Lindsay McKenna

A MAN ALONE

Silhouette®

SPECIAL EDITION™

Published by Silhouette Books

America's Publisher of Contemporary Romance

To all my faithful readers over the years—
you *are* the best!

SILHOUETTE BOOKS

ISBN 0-373-24357-X

A MAN ALONE

Visit Silhouette at www.eHarlequin.com

Printed in U.S.A.

Books by Lindsay McKenna

LINDSAY McKENNA

is a practicing homeopath and emergency medical technician on the Navajo Reservation. She lives with her husband, David, near Sedona.

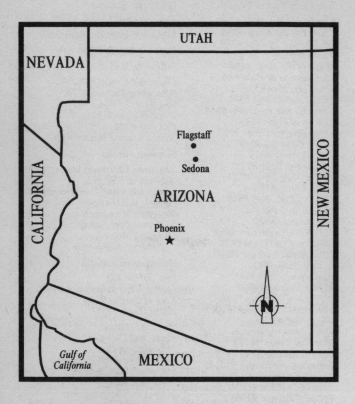

Chapter One

Two minutes until contact! The thought raced through Captain Thane Hamilton's mind, spurring him to run faster. Gasps tore from him. He was damn well going to make it, or else.

"Keep going!" he shouted hoarsely.

Ahead of him, a fourteen-year-old girl stumbled and ran brokenly. The hard desert terrain, the precipitous walls of the canyon surrounding them, were clearly taking their toll on her. And him.

With his desert fatigues, flak jacket and weapons, Thane's identity as a U.S. Marine was clear. Rifle in hand, he jerked a look over his shoulder. He knew the drug runners weren't far behind them.

There! Helicopters! Help was coming! Gripping the radio in his other hand, he growled at the floundering teenager. "Move it, Valerie!"

The red-haired girl sobbed and flailed her arms like an off-balance windmill in order to keep from slipping and falling on the unstable surface, strewn with gray and cream rocks.

Thane felt sorry for the senator's daughter. But it was necessary to keep her going. She was slowing, winded by the mile-long run. The sun was high, making him squint as he watched her in front of him. The canyon they ran in was just inside Bolivia's borders, and his lungs burned from the brutally high altitude. Sweat rolled down his face. The rest of his Recon team was dead. They'd risked five lives to rescue one girl. Thane was the last of his team. And he might not survive, either.

The sky was blindingly blue. He could hear the approaching "spook"—CIA-owned—helicopters, coming their way. Their rotors punctuated the air like a boxer punching him in the ears, the flat, chopping sounds reverberating through the area. At a prearranged checkpoint, he and Valerie were to be picked up. Up ahead, a desert plain appeared just beyond the mouth of the steep-walled, snakelike canyon. The helos would land only if he signaled them. The crew on the helicopters were expecting to rescue five people— and now there were only two. Thane wanted to cry. His team—his men—were dead, killed in that violent confrontation at a drug lord's estate.

"Move it!" he snarled.

Valerie sobbed. "I can't! I'm tired! I want to stop and rest!" She gave him a pouty look and started to slow down.

Cursing softly, Thane jammed the radio into his web belt. Surging forward, he gripped the girl's thin, flabby arm. She was a soft *norte americana* used to living the good life. She had a rich and powerful daddy in Washington, D.C. And even at such a young age, she was already a snob. Well, she was in over her head on this one. Oh, it wasn't Valerie Winston's fault that she'd walked ignorantly into a drug lord's carefully planned trap. She'd been with a church group, touring Machu Picchu in Peru, when she'd been kidnapped. Thane couldn't be angry at her.

"Ouch!" she shrieked, trying to yank away. "You're hurting me!"

Towering over her at six foot four inches compared to her five foot two, he nailed her widening hazel eyes with his own sharp gaze. "Tough it out, little girl. You and I are making that checkpoint. Now stretch those legs of yours. If you don't, we're dead meat. Is that what you want? A bullet in your back? Your brains splattered all over the rocks here?"

Defiant tears shimmered in her eyes. Her hair, long and naturally curly, hung about her shoulders, wild and uncombed. "No!"

Hamilton practically lifted her off her feet, steadied her on the rocky surface, then pushed her ahead of him at a faster clip. "Then move!"

It was June in Bolivia. Winter. And at fourteen thousand feet, colder than hell. His breath exploded out of his mouth in white clouds even though the noonday sun burned overhead. Lake Titicaca was only thirty miles away, the largest lake in the world despite the ungodly altitude. Thane heard the helos laboring mightily, the rotors grasping for oxygen that

wasn't there. That alone made flying up here to rescue them decidedly dangerous.

Thane had no idea who was going to pick them
up. He'd been told that a Boeing Apache attack helicopter and an old, antiquated Cobra from the Viet-
nam era were on this mission. Right now, he thought
as he jerked another furtive look across his shoulder,
he hoped it was the Apache that he heard in the distance. He needed that kind of firepower to protect
them from the oncoming drug runners.

With the echoing shouts of their assailants surrounding them, Thane and Valerie rounded the final
bend in the canyon. Above them were naked, barren
walls of yellow ocher and gray granite, weathered by
the fierce winds that scoured the Andes.

Gasping, his heart feeling like it was going to explode in his chest, Thane kept up the hard, pounding
pace. He heard Valerie sobbing. He knew she wasn't
used to this kind of demanding exercise. No one was
at this damnable altitude!

Thane saw the end of the canyon bleeding out into
a flatter area, a stark moonscape free of rocks, scrub
and trees. That must be the landing zone! The punc-
tuating rotors of the rescue helos lifted his hope. Behind, he heard shouts in Spanish. They were coming
closer.

Damn!

Turning, Thane saw ten drug runners hightailing
it in their direction, less than half a mile away. The
drug runners began firing. Turning on his heel, Thane
sped toward Valerie. Arms flailing weakly, she continued to run, all the while slipping and stumbling
on the rocky ground. He saw the helicopters ap-

proaching. Both were black. And both were coming in fast from high above, zeroing in like two attacking hawks on the landing zone below.

Jerking a canister from his web belt, he positioned himself directly behind Valerie. Bullets were whining all around them now, and ricocheting off the rock walls. Ducking as one screamed by his head, Thane kept himself between the girl and the drug runners. Under no circumstances could Valerie be hurt! They'd have to go through him and his Kevlar, bulletproof vest first.

Reaching the end of the canyon, he pulled Valerie against the rock wall.

"Stop," he rasped. Flipping off the handle to the smoke grenade, he lobbed it expertly toward the landing area two hundred feet in front of them.

The canister sailed through the air and plunked on the flat, yellow earth, which had hardened into a drumlike surface from lack of rainfall over the years. A puff of dust rose briefly as the canister bounced and came to a standstill. And then bright red smoke began to belch from it, forming thin, pinkish colored clouds. That was the signal for the choppers to land.

Turning, his nostrils flared, he brought the rifle up to his shoulder and sighted on the drug runners.

"Valerie, move to the right, but stay along the wall," he ordered.

The girl nodded jerkily, her eyes huge. She quickly moved away from him and crouched down, her back to the wall for protection.

The drug runners were going to catch up with them just as the helos landed, Thane realized. He squeezed off several shots to slow them, and it worked. Gripping the radio, he jammed the button down.

"Black Jaguar One. Black Jaguar One. This is Checkerboard One. Over." His breath came in gasps. His chest burned from overexertion. Sweat trickled into his narrowed eyes. He waited impatiently for a response from the big, black Apache that was thundering in toward the landing area.

"Come on!" he snarled. "Answer me!"

"This is Black Jaguar One, Checkerboard One," came a woman's low, steady voice. "What's your status? Over."

"A hot LZ," he warned. "I've got the package. And I've got ten bad guys, less than half a mile from us, comin' out of that canyon in front of you. I need some firepower. You got it? Over."

"Roger, we have them in our sights. Suggest you move back."

Stunned momentarily, Thane realized he'd been talking to a woman. A woman! Not a man, as he'd expected. And then, feeling stupid, he remembered that there were women Apache helo pilots in the U.S. Army. But behind the lines on spook-initiated missions? CIA? That, he'd never heard of. But now was not the time to ask questions or ponder the subject. "Read you loud and clear, Black Jaguar One. Thanks. You're a sight for sore eyes. Out."

Relief shuddered through Thane. He gave a tight, vengeful grin. Once that Apache released a deadly Hellfire missile into that bloodthirsty pack of cutthroats who wanted him and the girl dead, it would be all over. He silently thanked Boeing for making the battle-ready Apache. This aircraft, above all others, often made the difference between his team living or dying in behind-the-lines missions like this.

He saw the unmarked Apache "A" model helicopter suddenly lift upward and hover, preparing to take a shot at the drug runners. The second one, the old Cobra gunship, was coming in low and fast. Within thirty seconds, it would land. Glancing to his right, Thane saw Valerie crouched down into a ball of fright, her back to the wall, her arms tight around her drawn-up knees. Good, she was out of the way and protected.

His concern was the drug runners, who were moving at full speed toward him. Again, Thane snapped off five or six well-aimed shots. Two of the drug runners fell.

Then he spotted something that made his heart stop. *NO!*

Thane's green eyes widened enormously. Ahead of him, he saw that one of the drug runners had a LAW—a hand-held rocket launcher! And the bastard was aiming it directly at the hovering Apache, which was poised to fire.

Damn!

Thane leaped out from behind the wall, the thunder of the Apache deafening him as he exposed himself to his assailants' direct fire. He had to bring the drug runner down before he could launch that deadly rocket at the Apache! Kneeling down, Thane steadied his rifle. Bullets careened around him. He wore a protective bulletproof jacket, but that wouldn't stop a projectile from hitting him in the head. Counting on the drug runners' lack of marksmanship, Thane coolly aimed his rifle at the man who knelt with the rocket launcher pointed upward. No way was that bastard going to take down that helo! Squeezing the trigger, Thane felt the rifle buck solidly against his shoulder.

Before he could take a breath, he saw the bullet hit home, striking the man just as he launched the rocket. The man tumbled forward as the rocket launcher fired—directly at Thane!

Seconds slowed to a painful crawl. Thane gasped and thrust upward to his full height. *Escape!* He had to—*No! No! I'm going to die!* His last thought as he twisted to the left and dove for the safety of the rock wall was that he was a dead man.

Everything blacked out. The last thing he felt was a hot, burning pain in his right leg. The last thing he heard was Valerie's hysterical scream. And that was all.

"Oh, hell!" Captain Maya Stevenson yelled into the microphone against her lips. She instantly gripped the controls of the Cobra helicopter. "Dove, Angel, brace yourselves!" she warned her crew. Her emerald eyes narrowed as she saw the man in the canyon fire the rocket toward them.

And that Marine Recon was right in the way! Maya sucked in a breath, jammed her booted feet on the yaw-control pedals. She held the cyclic and collective in a choking grip. The wildly shot rocket exploded violently against the wall of the canyon. They were less than a quarter of a mile from it. In the danger zone.

The Marine Recon had to be dead!

The Cobra shook violently as the blast from the

explosion hit them. They were barely fifty feet above the ground with nowhere to go. Maya tensed. Dove, her copilot, sucked air between her clenched teeth. Angel, their gunner, whooped as the rocket exploded. Off to the left, Maya spotted their pickup, the senator's daughter. She appeared safe from the explosion. The Cobra skidded sideways from the concussion. Automatically, Maya worked to halt the awkward movement of the helicopter.

Above them, she heard the roar of two Hellfire missiles being released from the Apache's arsenal. In seconds, the entire canyon was filled with fire, dust and rocks flying in all directions.

"The bad guys are down, Major," Angel sang out with gleeful satisfaction.

"Yeah, but what about that marine?" Maya muttered. She landed the Cobra on the hard-packed desert floor. Dust whipped up in all directions around them. She shouted to Angel Paredes, "Go get the girl, Sergeant! We shouldn't receive any more resistance from the druggies. Stay alert!"

"Yes, ma'am!" Paredes leaped out of the helicopter. Short and stocky, she hustled around the nose of the Cobra and headed for the girl.

"Take over, Dove," Maya told her copilot. "And keep your eyes peeled."

"Where are you going?" Dove demanded, wrapping her long fingers around the controls.

Jerking at the snaps of her harness, Maya growled, "To look for that poor Recon bastard. He just saved Dallas and Cam from getting blown out of the sky. The least we can do is find his body and bring him home with us." She yanked out the cord that connected her with the communications system within the aircraft. Twisting around, Maya quickly made her way between the seats to the small cargo bay, past the fifty-caliber machine gun, and leaped off the lip of the shuddering helicopter. Dust was blowing in all directions, a small sandstorm around the aircraft. Maya drew her pistol, just in case she ran into one of the druggies in all the chaos. She made a sharp gesture with her hand toward her sergeant, who now had the girl beneath her arm.

"Get her on board!" Maya shouted above the noise.

Paredes raised her black-gloved hand to acknowledge the order before she hurried the girl toward the aircraft.

Turning, the captain ran toward the rock and rubble that had been left by the rocket's explosion. Although she had on her black helmet, with its protective black shield across the upper half of her face, the dust kicked up by the helo's blades whipped into her eyes. Rubbing them as she ran, holding her pistol high with her other hand, Maya tried to locate the marine among the piles of stone and dirt.

There! She saw the man lying on his back, his arms thrown outward from his unmoving body. Slowing, Maya looked ahead. Where the druggies had once been, rubble now covered half the width of the canyon. The bad guys were down and out. *Good. Instant burial. No formality.*

Kneeling down, Maya saw that the Marine's right leg, from below the knee, looked like ground, bleeding hamburger. She winced and clenched her teeth. Jerking off her black glove, she placed two fingers against the sweat-covered column of his throat. He was young and strong, but there was no way he could have survived this.

"I'll be damned," she breathed. She felt a faint pulse beneath her fingertips. It wasn't much of one— but it was there! Hurriedly, she assessed him for more wounds. The only place he seemed to be injured was his right leg. Holstering her pistol, she jerked off all his heavy gear and tossed it aside. She'd have to carry him to the helicopter. Judging from the amount of blood spurting from a cut artery in his calf, he was going to bleed to death—and soon.

Grunting, Maya turned him over and then rolled the weight of his body against her shoulder.

"You would have to be tall," she growled. Well, she was, too. Maya was thankful for her large-boned, six-foot frame because she'd never be able to hoist the marine into a fireman's carry position across her shoulders otherwise.

Just as she labored to get her feet under her, she saw Sergeant Paredes running full tilt toward her.

"Angel!" Maya yelled. "Get back to the helo! He's bleeding to death! Get an IV set up! I'm gonna need your help! Pronto!"

The sergeant skidded to a halt, nodded and sprinted back to the Cobra.

Groaning, Maya cursed softly as she placed each booted foot carefully in front of the other. He was heavy! Well, Recons had to be tough and hardy to do the work they did. Gripping him tightly by one arm and one leg, Maya swayed, fighting to keep her balance. Only a few more yards to go!

After setting up a temporary stretcher across the

steel-plated deck, Angel reached out from the lip of the helo. Maya groaned as she sat down with her load. When the sergeant angled the unconscious marine off her shoulders, Maya turned and helped to place the man on the awaiting stretcher. She saw the senator's daughter looking on, terror in her eyes as she sat huddled in one corner.

Leaping on board, Maya quickly slid the door shut. Turning, she moved between the seats and made an upward, jerking motion with her thumb. That told her copilot to get the hell out of here. To get some air between them, the ground and the bad guys. Though the druggies looked like they'd been buried under that rubble, she wasn't taking any chances.

Plugging the phone jack from her helmet into a wall outlet, she turned to help the paramedic-trained sergeant.

"I need help!" Angel gasped. "He's bleeding out! Captain...put your hand there! Now!"

Just then, the Cobra powered up, breaking gravity with the earth. Maya wasn't prepared and lurched downward onto her knees. Cursing in Spanish, she threw out her hands, palms slamming into the cabin wall just above where the marine lay. Despite the jostling and jerking, Angel was expertly pulling an IV from the black paramedic bag she kept on board.

Maya looked at the soldier's right leg. "Man, this is a mess, Angel," she said, addressing the sergeant by her nickname. Her real name was Angeline, but they called her the Angel of Death for many reasons, most of all because she was very good at pulling

Maya's wounded crews back from the jaws of death with her paramedic skills.

"I don't care *what* he looks like. Just get your hand on that bleeder," Angel rasped in Spanish. "Do it! Pronto!"

The captain had no trouble finding the artery that was spurting blood like a fountain. Jerking off her black glove, Maya grabbed a protective latex one from Angel's medical bag and quickly put it on. She hated to touch the marine's mangled right leg. She could see bone fragments mixed with the torn muscles, and the whiteness of a tendon that had been shredded by the blast.

"Geez, this is *bad*," Maya murmured sympathetically as she laid her hand over the exposed and cut artery.

"Yeah, well, if you'd just taken a direct hit from a rocket to your leg, you'd look like this, too."

Maya grinned darkly as Angel quickly hung the IV and inserted the needle into the marine's arm. "Don't get testy with me, Sergeant," she said, knowing Angel always got this way during a crisis. But Maya also knew Angel was an extraordinary woman, a Que'ro Indian, the last of the Inca bloodlines in Peru. Maya had wanted no one but this young woman, who had joined her top secret mission three years ago, to be on her aircraft with her. The Angel of Death had saved a lot of lives. She fought with her heart and soul to keep them alive.

Growling under her breath, Angel quickly jerked some thick, sterile dressings out of her pack. Paper flew in all directions as she ripped open the containers and got the sterile gauze out for use.

"Put these under your hand," she ordered Maya briskly. "And press down *hard.* A lot harder than you're doing right now. You want this guy to bleed to death on me? No way. He's *mine.* I'm not letting him go over yet...."

Blood from the marine's leg was pooling all over the deck. Maya felt the Cobra leveling out. They were gaining altitude.

"Get us out of Bolivia's airspace as soon as you can, Dove," she told her copilot. "And stay low, below their radar. If they find us over here, we're gonna hear about it at the U.N." By mutual accord, the U.S. had agreed not to invade Bolivia's airspace in their quest to stop drug smugglers flying across Peru's border. Well, too bad. What they didn't know wouldn't hurt them. Besides, Maya thought with her usual sick humor, their job at the Black Jaguar Express was to keep cocaine shipments from leaving Peru. If the effort spilled into Bolivia's sacred airspace from time to time, too bad.

Besides, they'd have to catch them at it to prove it, and Bolivia didn't exactly have a modern air force or state-of-the-art radar to prove their precious border had been encroached upon from time to time. Maya glanced down at the marine. Her heart squeezed in sympathy. "Can you save him?"

"Humph. I'm not a doc." Angel added more thick dressings to the bleeder.

"Stop hedging with me. You know about these things."

"He'll loose his leg, but he'll live. Okay?"

Maya nodded. "Too bad about that leg. He's a nice looking guy—for a marine."

They both laughed. Both of them were in the army, and there was always good-natured rivalry between the army and the other military services.

"Yeah," Angel rasped as she pulled a hypodermic needle from her pack and eyed it closely, "I wouldn't throw him out of bed for eating crackers."

Maya heard Dove laughing along with them. Their jobs were highly dangerous. On any given day, they could die. Dark humor was always their foil against their feelings, against the adrenaline rush pounding through them. It kept the terror they felt at bay so it didn't overwhelm them or their ability to think clearheadedly in such a crisis. Relief was threading through their fear now, beginning to ease the tension that had inhabited the aircraft moments earlier.

"Somehow, I can't see you hookin' up with a jarhead," Maya drawled.

Everyone laughed—a laugh of relief. Jarhead was a term army folk used to describe a marine—they just never said it to a marine's face if they didn't want a punch thrown their way.

"As good-lookin' as he is," Dove said, laughing over the intercom, "he's probably got a wife and a bunch of kids."

Maya grinned and nodded. They were going home to safety. Soon enough, they would be heading to their mountain base complex hidden deep in the Peruvian mountains. But first they'd have to fly to Cusco, the nearest large city, and have an emergency medical team take this marine into surgery to try to save his life. Maya and her crew had done this so many times before that the hospital staff in Cusco no longer asked who or what they were. Flying around in black, unmarked helicopters, wearing black, body-fitting uniforms, helmets and highly polished leather military boots, these women were an enigma to those who saw them. The hospital officials no longer asked about them, they simply allowed them to offload their wounded, give their names and a contact number of someone in a high government office in Lima, the capital, before they left for parts unknown.

As Maya knelt there, holding the thick, blood-soaked dressings over the marine's leg, she saw color starting to ease back into his pale, sweaty face. "I think he's coming to," she warned Angel.

"That's okay...I've got him on morphine. He ain't gonna feel a thing. Don't worry, he won't put up a fight."

"Good," Maya rasped as she watched the man's dark, short lashes move. Angel didn't always get painkillers into her patients soon enough, and they came back to consciousness swinging and fighting. And in a small helo like this, there wasn't much space to dodge flying fists. Maya positioned herself so she could face him. He'd be groggy, in deep shock, and probably not very coherent around his surroundings. Reaching out, she gripped his blood-ied, scraped left hand and held it firmly in her own. Angel quickly traded places with her in order to work on his leg, trying to sterilize it as best she could. Maya leaned closer to the marine.

The noise in the cabin of the Cobra was ferocious. Dove had redlined the engine to full throttle. The aircraft was old and shook like an old dog on trembling legs as it flew powerfully toward Cusco. Below them, the green velvet cape of the jungle spread outward. They were down below ten thousand feet and were beginning to wind among the loaf-shaped mountains clothed in green raiment. Wispy white clouds that always clung to the mountains blew like smoke across the windshield of the speeding aircraft.

"You're alive," Maya shouted near his ear. "Just take it easy. We've got the senator's daughter on board. You're both safe." She squeezed his hand to drive home her words.

His eyes opened slightly, to reveal murky-looking green depths.

Maya held his vacant stare. His mouth opened, then closed. His pupils were huge and black—from the hit of morphine Angel had just shot him up with. *Good.* He didn't need to know what had happened to his right leg. The marine blinked twice. She saw more awareness coming back to him. He had a strong mouth, and was used to being obeyed when he spoke, she was sure. There was nothing on his uniform to indicate his rank, but she knew instinctually that he was an officer.

"You're safe. You're on board my helicopter. We have your girl with us. She's safe, too. Hang on. We're flying you to Cusco, to a hospital there. You're in stable condition." That was a lie, but Maya didn't want the marine freaking out if he learned the truth of his fragile medical state.

There was so much noise in his head that Thane could barely make out what the woman leaning close to him in the black, tight-fitting uniform was saying. Where was he? His mind was spongy and refused to work properly. He felt like he was half out of his body. Floating. She was wearing a helmet. She must be a pilot? Not a soldier, no… His mind searched. What? Yes. That was it. Helicopter. He was in a helo. He could feel a familiar shaking and shuddering going on around him. He could feel the constant sensation all though his back and limbs…except for his leg. His right leg. Why couldn't he feel anything there? He could feel the shivering everywhere else.

Looking up into her face, Hamilton saw the grim set of her full mouth, the narrowed look in her eyes. She was a warrior, no doubt. There was a dangerous glint in her emerald eyes, too. The look of a hunter. Yet, for a moment, Thane saw something else in those slitted, feral eyes. What? He opened his mouth to speak.

"Captain Hamilton…" he croaked. The taste of mud was in his mouth.

She nodded. "Okay…good…we know who you are now." On missions like this, the Recons wore no identification of any kind, not even their dog tags. "We'll contact the proper authorities, Captain. I'm Captain Maya Stevenson, army spook pilot. You just hang on. We might look like a ragtag bunch, but believe me, you're in the *best* of hands." She grinned a little.

He tried to smile. He felt the strength of her hand around his. She was surprisingly strong—a big-boned woman, at least six feet tall, who was strong and confident. Right now, he needed that kind of reassurance. Thane became aware of another person. His eyes widened a bit. There was another woman, dressed in a similar black uniform, bent over his legs. She was putting white bandages on him. Funny, he couldn't feel anything down there. What was going on? When he tried to lift his head, the captain gently pressed her hand on his shoulder and kept him lying down.

"Whoa, Captain. You're in no shape to go anywhere. We want you to lie still, hear me? That's my paramedic down there, Sergeant Angelina Paredes."

His mouth was so dry it felt as if it would crack. He was thirsty. Barely moving his head to the left, he saw the red-haired girl. It took long moments to place her. His mind wasn't working worth a damn. Closing his eyes, Thane let out a trembling breath of air from between his bloody, bruised lips.

"Thank God, she's safe...."

Maya smiled and nodded. "You did good, Captain. You're a real hero. None of us thought you'd survived that direct rocket hit. You're one tough son of a bitch, for a marine." Maya saw one corner of his mouth rise at her teasing comment. She felt heartened. Maybe this guy was going to make it, after all. Still, his blood loss was horrific. And her sergeant was working like a wild woman over his mangled, continually bleeding leg. Right now, the last thing Maya wanted this heroic officer to know was that his leg looked like hell and there was every reason to believe that, once they reached Cusco, the surgeons would remove it.

That was heartbreaking to her. A man like this, who had incredible courage, would now became an amputee. He didn't deserve such a reward, Maya thought. Looking up at the girl who huddled in the corner, her eyes huge with tears, Maya felt for her, too. Life was nasty sometimes. Valerie Winston would never forget this. And Maya hoped she would never forget the men who had given their lives to rescue her. People like Captain Hamilton made the world a little better place to live in. A safer place for people like Valerie.

Leaning down, her lips close to his ear, Maya said, "Just try to rest, Captain. We're going to be landing in Cusco in less than thirty minutes. I've got the best paramedic in the world taking care of you."

Thane forced out the words. "Thank you…for everything."

Angel looked up momentarily, her lean, angular, dark brown face tense, the corners of her full mouth pulled flat. Her hands were bloody as she wrapped his injured leg.

Maya looked down at the marine once more. He had lost consciousness again. That was good. "It's sad, Angel. This guy deserves medals and it looks like he's going to lose this leg instead as a reward for what he just did."

"I dunno," Angel rasped as she reached around Maya and dragged her paramedic pack toward her. "If Dr. Del Prado is the bone surgeon on duty there at the Cusco hospital, he *might* try and save this dude's leg. He's got the ability to do it, but he's the only one in Peru who could pull it off."

"Better hope our best bone doctor is on duty, then," Maya said grimly.

"Captain?"

It was her copilot, Dove Rivera.

Maya lifted her head and looked toward the cockpit. "Yeah?"

"I'm receiving a top secret message for you, Captain. It's from Rolling Thunder. You expecting something from them?''

"Yeah..." The mission they were currently on was run by Perseus, a covert agency that often collaborated with the government. "That has to be the head of the organization, Morgan Trayhern. This mission was his ops—operation." She had never met Trayhern, but had worked with other officials within Perseus because it, too, operated in conjunction with the CIA, as did her base and operation in Peru.

"Oh, okay. Want me to patch it through to you over the private intercom?''

"Yeah, do it, Dove." Maya didn't care if her sergeant heard the message or not. They all had top secret clearances. Releasing the marine's limp hand, Maya pressed her fingers to the ear of her helmet to listen closely to the incoming message. Sometimes, such satellite transmissions were broken up, particularly in the mountainous regions of Peru where they were presently flying like a bat out of hell to save the marine.

"This is Kingbird to Rolling Thunder. Over," Maya said. Kingbird was their call designation indicator when satcom messages of this type had to be broadcast. In the event that anyone was able to capture the encrypted message, that person would have no idea of the caller's true identification or position at the time of the transmission.

"Rolling Thunder. Kingbird, have you got the goods? Over.''

The "goods" meant the girl, and Maya knew the code language. "Roger, we have the goods. Alive and well.''

"Roger. And Checkerboard? What is their status?"

Grimly, Maya knew that Checkerboard was the marine Recon team sent in to rescue Valerie. "Rolling Thunder, we have one survivor of Checkerboard. Right now, we are heading for the nearest hospital, where we have an emergency team on standby. Over."

"Roger. I will contact you when you arrive at your destination. Be on standby. Over."

"Roger that, Rolling Thunder. I'll await your call. Over and out."

"Rolling Thunder, out."

Maya watched as Angel placed a very tight tourniquet bandage around the bleeder, which seemed to have stopped leaking for the most part.

"That means we have to hang around for a call," Dove lamented.

Maya didn't like being on the ground wherever there were people and prying eyes. Especially in the second largest city in Peru. Because their mission was one of utmost stealth, top secret to everyone except two Peruvian government officials, she didn't like to draw attention to herself or her crews. "Yeah, I know. But Rolling Thunder wants the ID on this marine. He's going to have to contact his family and get him some medical help stateside. It's gotta be done."

"We'll stay with the Cobra," Dove said unhappily. "You gonna take the call inside the hospital?"

"Thanks," Maya said dryly, with a smile. She saw Dove's own smile as she turned her head briefly and met her eyes. Her copilot was also Que'ro Indian, from the highlands of Peru. She was only the second woman pilot in the Peruvian Air Force. Dove had turned into a fine helicopter pilot, thanks to training she'd received at Fort Rucker, Alabama, many years earlier. Now she was back in her own country to help the Peruvian people eradicate the drug trade. Nearly all her family had been murdered by drug lords, and she'd barely escaped with her young life. Dove Rivera had an ongoing vendetta against them, and with good reason. She lived to fly. She lived to kill every last one of them she could set her gun sights on. Maya didn't blame her.

"This guy's pressure is slowly dropping," Angel reported unhappily as she studied the reading on the blood pressure cuff. "Man...this isn't good. I was hoping he'd stabilize.... Del Prado isn't going to like this. The question is can we get him there in time or not?"

Maya slowly eased into a crouched position, because no one could straighten up fully within the tight confines of the helicopter. "Do the best you can," she soothed, and patted Angel's slumped shoulder. Picking up a nearby blanket, Maya made her way over to Valerie. The teenager was white-faced and scared looking. She needed to be held. The paleness of her freckled face, the darkness in her eyes, told Maya that much. Maya would play nurse-maid until they landed, and then Valerie would be turned over to awaiting U.S. government agents, who would whisk her into a private jet back to the U.S. and into her anxious father's waiting arms, no worse for wear—at least on the outside.

Smiling gently as she approached, Maya slowly

opened the blanket and slipped it around the girl's huddled form. She knew that she looked dangerous and threatening to the teen in her black uniform with the pistol at her side. A smile helped to ease the panic she saw in the girl's eyes. Valerie wasn't hooked up to the communications system, so she was unaware of what was being said or what was going down. The teenager was like a stranger in a strange place—a place where she had almost died.

As she knelt down in front of the girl and wrapped the blanket around her, Maya introduced herself and said, "Valerie, you're going home. You're safe now. We'll be landing in less than half an hour in Cusco."

Sniffing, Valerie wiped her eyes with trembling fingers. "Th-thanks. But what about Captain Hamilton? H-he saved my life. Will he live?"

Maya nodded and gave her a gentle smile. "I hope so."

"And his leg...oh, God...will he lose it?"

"Probably," Maya said, "but I don't know for sure."

Breaking into sobs, Valerie buried her face in her arms, her knees drawn up tightly against her thin, trembling body. All Maya could do was slide her arm around the girl's shoulders, pat her gently and let her cry.

Maya's thoughts drifted back to Hamilton. Maybe Rolling Thunder could do something to save this heroic marine's leg. She hoped so.

Chapter Two

"Is Captain Hamilton going to lose his leg?" Morgan Trayhern kept his voice low, but even he could hear the fear in it as he spoke with the bone surgeon, Dr. Jose Del Prado, in his office at the hospital in Cusco.

The physician, a wiry man in his early fifties, stood behind a simple mahogany desk in the spare white room. He was dressed in a long white coat, a stethoscope hanging out of his left pocket, and the report on Hamilton between his thin fingers. With a shrug, he said in stilted English, "I do not know...yet, Mr. Trayhern." He frowned, stroking his thin gray mustache.

Morgan grimaced. As soon as he'd heard the cryptic message from the spook helicopter rescue crew that had Hamilton and the senator's daughter safely aboard, Morgan had boarded the Perseus jet in Washington, D.C., and made a beeline for Cusco. Even though Captain Thane Hamilton was in the U.S. Marine Corps, and technically not working for him, the undercover assignment Hamilton had been on had been coordinated by Morgan and his company. Besides, Hamilton was a marine, as Morgan had once been himself. One never left a marine in the field. Not ever.

"I see...."

"No, *señor,* you do not." Del Prado's narrow face became intent. "I did not cut off his leg. I probably should have, to save him the agony he will surely endure not only physically, but emotionally. In the long term, it is my opinion that the officer will find that his leg is too painful to walk on. Right now, I am worried about long-term infection in his bones. If infection cannot be eradicated, he will lose his leg, anyway. Come, I will show you his X rays, so that you have a better understanding of what I did."

Morgan glumly followed the surgeon down a crowded hallway. The hospital, which was located in the second largest city in Peru, was busy. Every social strata intermixed within the polished halls of white tile flooring and dull green walls—from personnel clothed in white uniforms and lab coats to visitors dressed either in the native costume of the Que'ro Indian people or in the silk suits and fashionable winter dresses of the wealthy.

In the X-ray room, Del Prado quickly put up a series of pictures in front of the light boxes.

"These show Captain Hamilton's right leg." He pointed a slender finger at one X ray in particular as

Morgan, who was much taller peered over his shoulder.

"You can see, we have placed ten pins to try and get the bones to fuse back together."

His mouth in a grim line, Morgan stared at the X ray. "Looks like a damned mess in there."

Del Prado smiled a little. "Not exactly the medical terminology for it, but a good assessment, Señor Trayhern."

"So, what's next? May I transport Captain Hamilton in my jet, to continue his recovery at a stateside hospital?"

"Of course. He is stable now. You have a doctor on board to monitor him?"

Morgan nodded. "A trauma-trained emergency room physician. Yes."

"Then my suggestion would be to wait another twelve hours. He just came out of surgery three hours ago. We have him in a private room, as you ordered. He has just come out of anesthesia and is semiconscious. Give him time to adjust first."

"Would you suggest a bone specialist for him?"

"Of course. The infection in his bone, if it spreads, must be aggressively followed with antibiotics. And if the antibiotics do not oust it, then the infected part of the bone must be amputated. Otherwise, the infection will spread up his leg and eventually kill him."

Morgan nodded and sighed. Then he straightened and looked down at the prim doctor. "If he were your patient, what would you do for him?" When Morgan saw the doctor's blue eyes twinkle with laughter, he wondered what he'd said that was so amusing.

Del Prado's thin mouth puckered. "How we practice medicine here in Peru is a little different than what my colleagues practice in the U.S.A., *señor.*"

"Humor me, Doctor. What would you prescribe? They say you're the best hereabouts, so I'm very interested in your opinion and any ongoing therapy you'd recommend for Captain Hamilton. I'd like to see the man keep his leg. What's your secret to doing just that?"

With a flourish, Del Prado said, "I would combine standard medical treatment with alternative intervention. Maggots will eat away any gangrenous flesh that is bound to occur, create new blood vessel beds and bring oxygen into the tissue so it will live instead of die. Here in Peru we also utilize homeopathy, an alternative medicine widely known in Europe as well. I would, if he were to stay here, call in one of our staff homeopaths to work with me on the captain's behalf. We have found that homeopathy is an excellent support to traditional drug treatment, and the patient receives the best of both worlds. I would also suggest physical therapy along with massage. I know in your country that homeopathy and massage are not part of normal protocol for treating such a patient." He shrugged his thin, proud shoulders, his eyes gleaming. "But you did ask me what I would do, *señor.*"

"So I did. Thank you, Doctor. You gave me the information I needed. I want Captain Hamilton to have the best chance of saving his leg."

"Would you care for a referral to one of my *norte*

americana colleagues who studied for a year down here with me on just such cases?''

Again, Morgan saw the twinkle in the man's eyes. Realizing now that the doctor wasn't laughing at him, but rather introducing him to knowledge he knew to be foreign to most Americans, Morgan grinned a little in turn. ''Absolutely. Who do you suggest?''

''Dr. Jonathan Briggs, a doctor of osteopathy in Arizona who studied with our department a number of years ago. He's familiar with our protocols in a case such as your friend Captain Hamilton. He is a miracle worker of sorts in complex cases such as this. I can give you his address, Señor Trayhern. He practices out of the Red Rock Hospital in Sedona, Arizona.''

Nodding, Morgan said, ''This Dr. Briggs—will he use the same protocols you use?''

''*Sí.*''

''You're sure?''

With a terse laugh, Dr. Del Prado said, ''Dr. Briggs is the man who created this protocol for us in the first place.''

Grin widening, Morgan said, ''Thank you, Doctor. I'll see to it that Captain Hamilton ends up in Dr. Briggs's hospital.''

''*Bueno.* Good. You can go see Captain Hamilton now, *señor.* When you are ready, come to me and I will sign the captain's release forms.'' Del Prado escorted him out of the X ray room and into the hall. ''Captain Hamilton is on floor four, post-op. You will find him in room 404.''

Morgan shook his hand and thanked him. Turning,

he strode down the hall to the elevators carefully dodging swiftly moving nurses and orderlies.

Damn. Losing his leg will force Hamilton out of the Corps....

Morgan knew Hamilton's personnel jacket by rote. He made it his business to know the background of any person working on one of his operations. Morgan had never met the captain personally, or any of his Recon team, which had come out of Camp Reed, California, but that didn't matter. He knew the officer was a hard charger with an exceptional record of success on behind-the-lines missions. A man of action. Despite the fact that he was only twenty-seven years old, Hamilton was a marine of incredible accomplishment. And he was up for early promotion— major's leaves, too. As Morgan got off the elevator on the fourth floor, he wrinkled his nose. The smell of antiseptic was strong here. Almost overpowering. The scent always got to him, reminding him of the time he had spent healing in a hospital in a foreign country.

Fueled by that miserable memory, Morgan swore to get Hamilton out of here and somewhere familiar—somewhere he could heal surrounded by those who supported and loved him, if possible. As he walked down the empty hall and viewed the brass numbers on each wooden door he passed, memory of his injuries and the difficult time he'd had dealing with them alone convinced him that he did not want the same scenario for Hamilton.

Finding the correct door, he quietly nudged it open. The private room was small, whitewashed, the blinds on the one window closed giving the room a grayish, depressing look. He saw the young Marine Corps officer lying on a bed covered with white blankets, his face almost matching the material that surrounded him. His eyes were closed. His right leg was in a removable cast, lifted up by a series of pulleys and hung about a foot off the bed.

The odor of antiseptic made Morgan's throat tighten. Closing the door, he went over to the window, pulled open the blinds and swung the window outward. Fresh air from the city drifted in, though there was a hint of car pollution in it. He could hear the endless honking of horns below, but the sound was muted because the room was on the fourth floor. Despite everything, Morgan preferred a little fresh air to the choking smell of the hospital.

Turning, Morgan saw IVs in each of the officer's limp arms. As he moved toward the marine's bed, he saw his dark, spiky lashes flutter, his lids barely lifting to reveal murky green eyes with huge black pupils. From the way his eyes appeared, Hamilton was still coming out of the surgery anesthesia.

"Take it easy, Captain Hamilton," Morgan said as he approached the bed. "I'm your contact, Morgan Trayhern. I got down here as soon as I could when I found out you'd survived the mission." He lifted his hand and gently placed it against the white gown across the officer's shoulder. "Welcome back to the land of the living, Son. You're in Cusco, Peru, and you've just come out of surgery, three hours ago. How are you feeling? Any pain?"

Thane stared up at the tall man, noting vaguely the concern written across his broad, tense features. The silver gray at his temples shouted of his age, but to

Thane, he looked a lot younger and very fit in the charcoal-gray pinstripe suit, impeccably pressed white shirt and conservative, dark blue silk tie. His brain still slow at processing, it took long moments for Thane to understand everything the man had said. The warm grip of the man's hand on his shoulder, though, translated instantly, and Thane felt genuine care radiating from this stranger.

Opening his mouth, he realized it felt dry, like the Bolivian desert itself.

"Thirsty?"

He nodded slightly, feeling incredibly weak.

Morgan reached for a pitcher of water on the nearby stand, poured some into a cup and placed a straw into it. "Nurses been by to check on you yet?"

Thane sucked noisily on the straw. His mouth wasn't exactly in working order. Grogginess and a floating feeling made his thoughts tumble loosely. Whispering his thanks for the glass of water, he lay back, exhausted by the simple act of drinking and swallowing.

"Don't—remember...sir...." he said, his voice hoarse. His throat hurt. It was painful to swallow. Frowning, he looked around. There was an ache drifting up his right leg toward his thigh. What was wrong with it? Automatically, he weakly lifted his right arm to touch his right thigh beneath the thick blankets covering him. Frowning, he saw that his leg was lifted slightly and hanging from a series of pulleys at the end of the bed. It took him long moments to realize why his leg was hanging there like that.

And then, slowly, the reason for his leg injury came back to him. As the man beside his bed stood quietly, images of the mission formed before Thane's shut eyes. The sounds. The loss of his team. The girl, Valerie. And…a woman's face. She was dressed in a tight-fitting black flight uniform with absolutely no insignias anywhere on it. She hovered over him, a worried look on her beautiful face. A helicopter…yes, he remembered being in a shaking and shuddering helo. And his leg. *No*…. Somewhere in his drugged, spacy mind, Thane recalled another woman in a black uniform saying he was going to lose his leg. *No!* Panic surged through him. As it did, it began to wipe away his semiconscious state. The floating sensation was erased by the surge of adrenaline now flooding his bloodstream.

"Easy, Son…."

Thane opened his eyes. His leg was still attached. Wasn't it? He was breathing hard now, his chest rising and falling with effort. Reaching out with his right arm, alarmed at how weak he was, he clawed at the covers near his knee.

"You still have your leg."

Relief shuddered through him and Thane ceased his efforts to see if his heavily swathed and bandaged limb was really there or not. He couldn't feel his leg, just the ache throbbing upward from it. A groan emitted from his parted lips as he fell back on the pillows. Heart pounding heavily in his chest, he knotted his right hand into a fist.

"My leg…" Thane felt Trayhern's hand tighten briefly on his shoulder, as if to reassure him. He desperately needed that small act of kindness right now.

"From the after-action report I received, Captain Hamilton, they said a rocket launcher was fired. Apparently, according to the approaching helo rescue team, you dived behind a wall just in time. The rocket exploded into the rock just in front of you. I'm sure you don't have memory of that—yet.''

Thane weakly moved his head from side to side. All he cared about, all he wanted, was to know that his right leg was still a part of him. The person on the helo had been wrong, thank goodness. He couldn't stand the thought of not being whole. Not being able to go back to the Corps and be a career officer.

Nostrils flaring, he tried to settle down. His emotions, he discovered, were like the wild horses of Arizona that he'd once seen on the ranch where he'd grown up. Focusing his eyes on the somber looking man named Trayhern, he held his dark blue, penetrating gaze.

''My leg? What else?''

''According to the surgeon, they're worried about infection.''

''Don't let them take it....''

Morgan squeezed his shoulder again and felt the powerful muscles beneath the gown Hamilton wore. The man was in top shape. As a Recon Marine, he'd have to be. ''We're going to do everything in our power to see that you keep your limb, Captain.''

Panic seized Thane. ''You mean...I might lose it?'' *No! No, that can't happen!* His heart raced with anguish as more and more of his drug-induced state was wiped out by another surge of adrenaline.

Morgan held up his hand. ''I've got an idea, Captain. I need to make some phone calls. When I come back, I'll have more answers and a plan of action for you. I'm going to do everything in my power to make sure you keep that leg.''

Thane closed his eyes. Pain was now drifting up his leg into his thigh, and knotting his gut. He bit back a groan. ''I *won't* lose my leg—sir,'' he declared between clenched teeth. ''Hell will freeze over before I allow anyone to cut it off....''

Morgan saw the dangerous glint come into the younger man's eyes, the black pupils constricting and a look of stubbornness entering. Lifting his hand, Morgan said, ''No one wants to see you walking on two legs more than me. I'll be back, Captain.''

Thane was completely conscious the next time Morgan Trayhern came in, an hour later. The nurse had him sitting up, and had given him an IV drip of morphine for the after-surgery pain, but he was much more alert. The nausea in his stomach had abated, for which he was grateful. His gaze kept going back to his right leg. Dr. Del Prado had come in less than fifteen minutes ago and given him the prognosis. He didn't leave much hope that he'd keep it in the long term. That scared Thane. Scared him a lot.

He looked up eagerly as Trayhern walked toward him. The man was ex-military, no question. And Hamilton knew the legend about him. Every marine did. The fact that Morgan had been a marine was a godsend. Marines always took care of their own, and it was apparent that Trayhern was going to do the same for him. That gave Thane hope despite the brutal words of the Peruvian doctor.

''Things are set into motion, Captain Hamilton,''

Morgan informed him as he halted at the side of his bed.

Thane felt a semblance of relief and released a breath of air from between his tightly compressed lips. Somehow, Trayhern's husky words, the look in his dark blue eyes, reassured him. "What's in motion, sir?"

He smiled a little. "Several things. Just lie back and relax, Son, and I'll fill you in on what we're going to do."

Morgan saw the hope in the man's tense features. There was more color flooding into his face, making his cheeks look ruddy. The eaglelike alertness in his dark green eyes settled directly on him. Hope filtered through Morgan as he laid out the plan.

"I'm taking you stateside on a Perseus-owned jet that's being readied at the Cusco airport. I have a trauma physician on board who will monitor you all the way back. We're landing at the Sedona, Arizona, airport, where you'll be met by an ambulance. You'll be taken directly to the Red Rock Hospital. I've talked to their head bone doctor, Jonathan Briggs, who's one of the best in the nation, according to Dr. Del Prado." Morgan smiled a little, triumph in his tone. "I talked personally to Dr. Briggs just a little while ago and he's willing to take you on as a patient. Not only that, but I've talked to your mother, Judy Hamilton, to let her know that you're all right and you're coming home. At this same hospital, they have one of the best physical therapists in the state. And a masseuse who works with this therapist. I've also contacted a local homeopath, Rachel Donovan-Cunningham, who has agreed to work with you on your case. Dr. Briggs has no problem using alternative medicine right along with standard treatment. He'll be reviewing your records and X rays as soon as we get you to the hospital."

Morgan saw the man's eyes flare with shock, though he didn't understand why. He added, "Dr. Briggs is one of the best bone surgeons in the U.S.A. The very top. I wanted you in the best of hands, Captain Hamilton. I didn't want you put in a military hospital somewhere. I know you were probably expecting that, but since you're on our payroll and it was our mission, you're not obliged to go to military hospital. We pay for everything, if that's what has you worried. I take care of my people, Captain. They get the best. And wherever the best are located, that's where you go to heal. The fact that your hometown is Sedona, is a lucky stroke. But it doesn't take away from the fact that Dr. Briggs is there and that's where I'd put you, anyway."

Morgan smiled a little, pleased with the way things were falling into place. "Besides, your mother was thrilled with the idea that you would be so close to home. In my experience, having family around, people who love you, is an asset in a long-term war of recovery, Captain. No one can guarantee you'll keep your leg—yet. And I know the importance of family, loved ones and friends in a battle like this. All it can do is help you in the long run."

Stunned, Thane lay there taking it all in. He opened his mouth, then snapped it shut. What the hell was he going to do? Knotting the material beneath his hands, he stared straight ahead. Hurt pumped through his chest with every beat of his heart. *Home*. Not exactly a word that he jumped up and down with joy over. And his mother...

His throat constricted as he rasped, "Sir, with all due respect, I don't need *home* in order to keep my leg."

Scowling, Morgan heard the edge in the man's low tone. He saw a flicker of emotion in his narrowed green eyes. Sensing something was wrong, Morgan stood there for a moment digesting the officer's tightly spoken words.

"Captain, I was once badly injured. When I came to, I was in a foreign hospital surrounded by people who spoke a language I didn't understand. I had *no one*. No family. No friends. I remember how alone I felt. How I cried at night in the darkness of that ward. For me, the pain of that was a helluva lot worse than the pain in my head and the rest of my body from the wounds I sustained. Looking back on that period of my life, I'm sure I'd have recovered far more quickly than I actually did, if I'd had people who loved me around."

Thane swallowed hard. Pain was arcing through his heart. It felt like a fist was surrounding the organ and squeezing it to death. His nostrils flared. He tried to squelch his feelings. It was no use. "There's got to be another bone doctor in the U.S. Isn't there, sir?"

Morgan heard the desperation in the officer's tone, saw it clearly in his taut expression. "Dr. Briggs is the best in the country. I want you in his hands."

Dammit! "Then, sir, I'll remain at the military hospital at Camp Reed, instead."

Tipping his head slightly, Morgan tried to ferret

out the truth behind the marine's tautly strung words. "When you have a home? A ranch to go to?" There was disbelief in his tone. He saw Hamilton struggle mightily with anger that flashed momentarily in his eyes. His mouth thinned considerably.

"You spoke to my mother, sir?"

The words were icy.

Disgruntled, Morgan said, "Yes. Why?"

"And she was ready to receive me with open arms?" Thane couldn't help the sarcasm dripping out of his mouth.

Uneasy, Morgan said, "Yes. She was, first of all, relieved that you were alive. And when I told her of my plan, she was the one who suggested that she could have your room turned into a makeshift hospital room once you are released from the Red Rock facility. In fact, she said her part-time housekeeper is working on the room as we speak. Clearly, you're upset, Captain. Care to clue me in on what's going down here?"

Anger drifted through Thane. His fists unknotted. He wiped the gathering beads of sweat from his furrowed forehead with a weak swipe of his right hand. Breathing hard, he glared up at Trayhern.

"Family differences, sir."

Morgan knew that whatever the problems, they weren't any of his business. "Your mother gave no hint of any 'problems,' Captain. And based upon that, one of my assistants is working directly with her to get your old bedroom ready to receive you when you get out of the hospital."

"Sir...I'll go anywhere other than *home* when I

get out of the hospital.'' Thane nailed Morgan with a deadly look. ''Anywhere but there.''

Morgan grimaced. *Great.* He hadn't anticipated this. ''I'll see what I can do, Captain. No guarantees, however. Dr. Del Prado made it clear to me that you were going to need twenty-four hour care once you were out of the hospital. I happen to think that home is a helluva lot better place than some apartment. Besides, you're going to need a lot of help. Your mother said that the woman who works for her part-time also works at the hospital.''

''Who's that?''

Morgan grimaced. ''I think she said her name was Paige.''

''Paige?'' Thane closed his eyes. He remembered that name from his high school days. A beautiful, shadowy, mysterious girl named Paige Black. She was half Navajo and half Anglo. A scared little rabbit of a girl with long, black, shiny hair, a thin, graceful body. As he recalled she was so excruciatingly shy that she always walked with her head down so she wouldn't have to make eye contact with anyone.

''Paige Black, by any chance?'' he demanded.

''Yes…I think that's her last name.'' Morgan cleared his throat. ''Paige would be charged with your daily care, Captain. She's a registered nurse and a licensed masseuse. Your mother would not be in charge and she understands that. She approved of Paige taking up residence in her home while you are there. She said it wouldn't be a problem.''

Opening his eyes, Thane stared glumly up at the man. ''Anything would be better than my mother, sir.''

"I see...."

No, he didn't, but that didn't matter to Thane. He wasn't going to air his family's dirty laundry in front of Morgan Trayhern. Thane also knew he didn't have enough money to rent an apartment in Sedona for any length of time, as it was expensive real estate. Morgan was being more than patient and generous about this, and fortunate to get him a bone specialist like Briggs. Right now, keeping his leg mattered more to Thane than having to live under the same roof with his mother.

"I can tolerate the situation if Paige Black is going to be my nurse and take care of me," he growled.

Morgan sighed internally. "I'm glad to hear that, Captain. Like I said, it has been my experience that home is the best place to heal."

Not in his view, Thane thought, but he didn't argue. "Thank you, for everything. I'm tired now, sir. I need to sleep."

"I understand. Take a nap, Captain. My assistant is getting everything ready for a departure at 0600 tomorrow morning. We'll be landing back on U.S. soil five hours after takeoff." He squeezed the officer's shoulder. "You're in good hands, so just relax."

After Trayhern left, Thane opened his eyes. He was tired, but he wasn't sleepy. His heart in turmoil, he looked out the window and heard the noise from the traffic below. The sky was a deep blue, with a few wispy clouds. It was around noon, from what he could make out.

"Dammit..."

His softly whispered words, filled with pain,

drifted eerily around the room. *Home.* He was going home. The last place he wanted to be. What kind of twisted fate did he have?

Moving his gaze angrily around the quiet room, Thane felt panic. He wanted to run. And then he laughed bitterly. Hell, he didn't even have two useful legs to run anywhere on! And now he'd have to face his mother. That prospect made his gut clench and knot. For years he had avoided his mother and the ranch where he'd grown up. Even though he craved to have someplace to call home, he knew that place wasn't with his mother. Oh, she had tried to instill the love of her family's ranch and the land into him, but he'd ferociously resisted it. And yet in times of quiet, which weren't frequent in his hectic life, his foolish heart would crave that place known as the Bar H. *Home.* And he'd catch himself and instantly deny he had any such longing. The Corps was his home, he reminded himself sternly.

His mind moved swiftly to thoughts of Paige Black. Instantly, his stomach unknotted. When Thane closed his eyes and pictured her soft, oval face, her skin that sunset-gold color that belied her mixed heritage, the thick, long folds of shining black hair that emphasized her high-cheekboned face, his heart settled a little. The panic he felt began to ease, too. In high school, Paige had been a shadow. Everyone had teased her and her two older sisters about being shy little rabbits. Oh, it wasn't right that they had been treated like that, but Thane knew why it had happened. The Navajo people too often suffered from prejudice, and since Paige and her sisters were part Navajo, they had been branded by the white kids.

Sighing, he realized that during his high school years, he'd always been more than a little aware of Paige's quiet, unobtrusive presence. He'd been too fearful to approach her, afraid she'd reject him outright because he was an Anglo. Not that he'd ever made fun of her. No, Thane's prejudice didn't run in that direction. Her large, liquid eyes had always reminded him of a beautiful, graceful deer, and he'd never forgotten them. He'd wondered, from time to time, what had happened to her. Well, now he'd find out because of fate. His life…his leg were being entrusted to her care.

She must have gone on to Yavapai College to become a registered nurse, he mused. He knew it was a nice little college with a satellite in Cottonwood, which was only thirty minutes away from Sedona. He was glad she'd made something of herself. In a way, he was surprised, because Paige had always been passive and shy. Four years of college required a lot of persistence. Somewhere beneath that quiet, graceful demeanor, she had a backbone of steel, and that made him grin with pleasure.

The Blacks had a small ranch, he recalled, a struggling one where they raised sheep to produce wool for their large extended family, most of whom still lived on the reservation. The Black family was renowned for their Navajo rugs, which were sold for very high prices around the world. Those rugs brought money so the whole family could survive. But a Navajo family was large and extended, and the money never went far enough. Everyone had made fun of Paige's parents having a ranch off the res. But conditions in the Sedona area were perfect for raising sheep. Back then, it wasn't accepted that Navajo could survive off their reservation. But the Blacks had, out of pure guts and perseverance. Thane respected the hard-working family for that. They worked twelve hours a day, a hardscrabble existence, but they had succeeded.

What did Paige look like now? Thane wondered. Life had taken them in very different directions. He'd gone on to Annapolis at age eighteen and into a career as a marine officer. He had wanted to follow the illustrious footsteps of his father, who had been a Marine Corps general.

Scowling, Thane remembered how his mother had divorced his father when Thane was only twelve years old. She'd wanted to go back to her family's ranch to raise him. She'd wanted a steady place for him to grow up and become a young man rather than be shunted like a Ping-Pong ball from one Marine Corps base to another every two years. Bitterly, Thane recalled the nasty divorce and the judge making a decision that, yes, he would go to Arizona to live with his mother until he was eighteen.

Thane had always hated that decision. Hated his mother for divorcing his larger-than-life father. Thane felt once more the white-hot grief of being separated from his dad, whom he adored and took after in every way. He hated the years spent at the cattle ranch because he had only been able to see his father once a year—if he was lucky. His dad had been overseas for three of those painful years of separation, and during that time Thane never saw him at all. It left a big wound in him, a lot of anger toward his mother. She had no right to do what she'd done.

Thane could never understand her reasons or her dreams. Or her.

But then, he reminded himself bitterly, he didn't exactly have a great track record when it came to understanding women, anyway. Too many of them reminded him of his mother in one way or another, and that scored the still-open and bleeding wound deep within him.

Home…I'm going home. What a hell of a fix. What was he going to do? His mother was fifty-eight years old now. He hadn't seen her in ten years. Then, two years ago, his father had died unexpectedly of a heart attack. Thane had seen her at his funeral in Washington, D.C. and had spoken stiltedly to her. She had pleaded with him to settle their differences and be a family once again, but he'd steadfastly refused. His father had died a lieutenant general in the Marine Corps, a man widely respected and well loved by those in his command. Thane tried to mirror him in every way. He'd loved his father deeply. And seeing his mother at the funeral only exacerbated his grief over his father's passing.

"Damn…." he rasped.

The word echoed weakly around the silent room.

Only the fact that Paige Black would take care of his needs on a daily basis made going home anywhere near palatable. Thane felt like he had been thrown from the skillet into the fire. And yet his only objective while riding this emotional maelstrom was saving his leg and getting the hell out of his mother's house as soon as possible, going back to work as a marine. Above all, he wanted his old job back. And one way or another, he was going to accomplish it. Nothing else mattered. Nothing.

Chapter Three

Thane spent his time on the Perseus jet that flew him back toward the States writing letters of condolence to the wives and families of the men he'd lost on the mission. It was a task demanded of him because he was the officer in charge of the Recon team. Even if it hadn't of been, he'd have written. These men were his friends; they were like younger brothers to him. His handwriting was shaky and his eyes filled with tears again and again, until he was done. Sometime after that, with his hands folded over the last letter he'd written, he fell into an exhausted sleep.

At some point, someone gently removed the heartfelt letters from beneath his hands, which rested on his blanketed stomach. It might have been Jenny, the trauma physician, or Morgan himself. Thane wasn't sure, but it didn't matter. Both were from the military and he knew they understood.

When he awoke, they were within an hour of their destination. Morgan was up in front, speaking on a phone, at a makeshift desk with papers surrounding him. The rear of the Lear jet had been revamped to make it easy for patients like Thane, who lay on a gurney with tubes hanging out of him, to ride with relative ease. Pain had awakened him. Jenny, who was in her mid-thirties, with short red hair and sparkling green eyes, adjusted the IV drip to give him more painkiller to ease his discomfort.

As soon as she did, Thane lapsed once more into a deep, almost comalike sleep. He was sure his need to sleep was due to many things: his injuries, the trauma of the surgery, his escalating emotions and grief over the loss of his men, his concern over what these losses were doing to the families, among other things. And, beneath it all, lay something he didn't look at very closely: the fact that he was going home to a mother who was more a stranger to him than a parent. And to a house he'd hated growing up in because he'd considered it a prison. The weight of all those emotions raged through him, unchecked.

The next time Thane woke up, he found himself in a pale pink room. It took him a few minutes to realize that he was in a hospital—more than likely Red Rock Hospital, in Sedona, Arizona. It was a far cry from the Cusco hospital. This room was cheery in comparison, with fuschia venetian blinds, green plants hanging near the window and several paintings of flowers and landscapes. His leg was suspended, once again, with a set of pulleys and he noticed he wore a pair of light blue pajamas. The bed covering was a deep fuschia color and matched the venetian blinds. To his left was a huge set of windows, and he could see he was on the ground floor. There were shiny-leafed pyracantha bushes along the bottom edge of the window. Beyond that, he saw the gorgeous spires and buttes of Sedona.

New emotions filtered through him as he gazed upon the red rock country where he'd grown up, noticing once more how the red sandstone was sandwiched between layers of white rock as it spiraled high into the dark blue sky. Turning his gaze from the late evening dusk that hung over the small community, he saw there were a number of bouquets of flowers in the room—bright red, rust-colored, yellow and pale lavender wildflowers from around the area. He would recognize these flowers anywhere and he welcomed their sweet scent over the antiseptic odor he'd encountered in the Cusco hospital. There was no mistaking that it was June in Sedona, for summer had come to this tourist town in all its colorful splendor.

The door to his room cautiously opened. Thane turned, his heart thudding hard in his chest. A young woman dressed in a pale blue smock and loosely fitting dark blue slacks, a stethoscope around her neck and a chart in her hands, moved quietly into the room. She gave him a shy, hesitant smile.

Thane recognized her at once. It was Paige Black. The fear that had knotted his stomach when he'd thought his mother had come to visit him dissolved instantly. A warmth flowed through him at the sight of her. How had she grown so beautiful? Her eyes were large and damp looking, as if she'd been crying recently. Yet the look in them welcomed him with undeniable warmth and recognition.

"Hi. I'm Paige Black, Captain Hamilton," she said uncertainly. "I was just coming to check on you, to see if you were awake yet. Your mother wanted to know so she could drive over and welcome you home."

Thane's eyes traveled over her from her head down to her toes, and back up to her face. Paige could barely hold his narrowed green gaze. She could feel his intense look sweep over her like a fire suddenly out of control, creating a burning sensation. Inwardly, she was trembling with joy as well as trepidation.

Thane swallowed convulsively. Paige was more beautiful than ever. He remembered her in high school, when she hadn't been half as pretty as she was now. Perhaps it was her height that gave her such a magnetic presence, for she stood about five foot seven inches tall. Her shining ebony hair was drawn back with a large sterling silver, turquoise-studded comb at the back of her head. She wore no makeup, but that didn't matter. Her thick, arched eyebrows set off her very large, cinnamon-colored eyes. When he saw her dip her head and avoid his eyes, he recalled belatedly that Navajo did not like to make eye contact with strangers. They felt it assaultive. Disrespectful. And he'd been staring at her like a starving wolf. Still, she stood there, her hands crossed in front of her, and patiently endured his inspection.

Clearing his throat nervously, Thane lifted his

hand, though he was still very weak. "Call me Thane, Paige. It's good to see you again." And it was. He hungrily absorbed her soft, placid looking features. Her skin was golden, her cheekbones high, her eyes slightly tilted to give her a look of mystery and intrigue. More than anything, her mouth looked delicious to him. Her lips parted in surprise when he talked to her in such a friendly manner. She lifted her head like a startled deer caught in headlights. Why?

"Y-you…remember me?"

Just the soft, husky tone of her voice soothed his jangled nerves and raw emotional state. Her eyes were huge with shock as she stared across the room at him.

He managed a brief, hoarse laugh. "Remember you? Sure I do. Why wouldn't I?" And indeed, why wouldn't he? Thane felt his heart beating rapidly in his chest. He found himself helplessly devouring the sight of this quiet, tranquil beauty. Everything about her spoke of peace and calmness.

Paige smiled gently and touched her cheek, which felt hot. "You have a wonderful memory, Captain—I mean, Thane…." Awkwardly, she clasped her hands again. How handsome he was! Paige tried to stop the old pain in her heart from leaking through her joy at seeing him once more. She'd never expected to see Thane Hamilton again after he'd left for Annapolis. If he knew that she'd had a crush on him in high school, he'd laugh himself silly. Now he was back here—with her. But not of his own free will.

Thane lay back, feeling suddenly joyous for no

discernible reason. Even the fear of his upcoming meeting with his mother melted away beneath Paige's warm brown gaze. "I never forgot you," he stated. And he hadn't. For him, she'd always been a mystery—an ethereal creature who was more a shadow than a reality in his life.

The huskily spoken words riffled across her aching heart. Paige tried to sternly tell herself that Thane was her patient, someone she would care for during his convalescence, but that was all. More heat rolled into her face. She placed her hands against her cheeks and looked away.

"I'm blushing like a teenager," she admitted, laughing breathlessly. "I guess our school days follow us around, after all."

His eyes narrowed speculatively at her. A part of her was still a child, even though she stood before him as a tall, graceful woman. "We have a lot in common," he told her, giving her a wan smile. "We went to the same high school for four years. I'm glad someone I knew then is taking care of me now, instead of a stranger."

Trying to gather her scattered, joyful emotions, Paige forced herself to take a more businesslike stance with him. She hadn't expected Thane to remember her. Or for him to say such wonderful words to her. Moving briskly, she came to his bedside.

"That's true, we did. But you were the superstar of Red Rock High School. I was a nobody." She was still a nobody, she thought as she checked the drips on the IVs feeding a painkiller and liquid nutrients drop by drop into an artery in each of his arms. "I work here full time as a registered nurse. I assist Dr. Malone, who is going to be your physical therapist. I'm also a licensed masseuse.'' She looked at the IVs closely, pretending to be busy with them. Paige couldn't stand the powerful masculine energy that surrounded Thane, energy as potent to her as sunlight. It always had been. Only now he seemed ten times more male, more powerful, to her. Paige felt panicked beneath his continuing stare. Was she so unattractive that he couldn't tear his gaze from her? Johnny had been abusive to her in every way. He said she was dog ugly, that her face was mis-shapen. Once he'd pointed out that one side of her mouth moved up more at the corner than the other side, that her left eye was slightly larger than her right one. Everything about her was out of balance, and according to the Navajo way, the beauty way, harmony and balance was the goal of life. Maybe that was why Thane was staring at her like that. He saw the disharmony of her features, too.

''I'm impressed with your credentials,'' he murmured. Paige was so close. So wonderfully close. He could smell the fresh outdoors on her, a slight, clean scent of sage. Her skin was a flawless dusky color, proudly proclaiming her mixed heritage. Her black lashes were thick and framed her sparkling eyes, which carried flecks of gold in their depths.

''Are you comfortable?'' she asked, moving back a step from his bed.

Thane nodded. ''As much as I can be. When did I arrive here? The last thing I remember is falling asleep on the plane about an hour from our projected landing time.''

''You got here an hour ago.'' Paige glanced at the

practical-looking watch on her slim wrist. "It's 4:00 p.m. now."

"And Morgan Trayhern? Is he still around?"

Paige shook her head. She was nervous around Thane. He was a large man, heavily muscled, and so very good looking. But, what had drawn her to him so many years ago was his sensitivity and care of others. He'd never been an egomaniac just because he was the star of the football team and had led their team to two state championships. Instead, he'd always talked about how each member on his team was a hero, how it was teamwork that allowed them to win. No, Thane had treated everyone equally. He never ran with a clique. And he'd been busy in several clubs at school as well, organizations that helped the poor and the elderly. Paige had loved him fiercely for his humanity, for his kindness to others who had less than he.

Realizing she hadn't answered his question, she stammered, "Uh, n-no. Mr. Trayhern left, but—" she turned and quickly moved to the dresser opposite his bed "—he left this for you." She picked up a thick manila envelope. Bringing it to his bedside, she said a little breathlessly, "And he said to tell you that the letters you wrote would be sent off tonight to the families, and not to worry about the details. He'd take care of everything, including sending flowers for the funerals, which will be held shortly."

Thane frowned and took the envelope. "I see. Thanks...."

Paige saw the pain and grief in his eyes. His mouth moved into a thin line. She fought the urge to touch him, to comfort him as he grieved at the terrible loss

of his men. "I…I heard what happened. Mr. Trayhern said you're a hero. I'm sorry for the loss of your
team, Thane." It was impossible not to reach out,
and so Paige risked everything, tentatively placing
her fingers across his muscular forearm, covered with
soft, dark hair.

Just the soothing, cooling contact of her fingers on
his skin eased some of his pain. Thane saw her eyes
fill with genuine care and sadness. He knew Navajo
custom was that once someone died, that person was
never spoken of again. Of course, in his world, things
were different. But right now he didn't want to talk
about his friends. Maybe the Navajo had the right
idea, after all. "Thanks," he said, his voice rough
with tears, despite how he fought the emotion he felt.
Overwhelming grief surged up through his chest, creating a huge lump in his throat. He swallowed re-
peatedly and tried to contain his feelings.

"Is there anything I can do for you?"

Thane shut his eyes. Her soft voice penetrated the
wall of pain he was barely holding on to. The firm-
ness of her cool fingers was steadying to him. Taking
in a jerky breath, he opened his eyes and stared
straight ahead.

"No."

The word came out flat and controlled. Paige's
hand left his arm. He felt bereft. Idiotically, Thane
wanted to cry out, throw his arms around her and
hold her tight against him, sobbing and screaming
out his pain against her soft, rounded breasts.

Stunned by that reaction, he withdrew deep inside
himself. He saw Paige step back. The look on her
face told him he'd hurt her with his blunt refusal of

her help. *Damn*. She was the *last* person he meant to hurt right now. Moving his mouth, he tried to apologize, but nothing came out. All he could feel was the grief that was ready to avalanche downward.

"Let me call Dr. Briggs. He wanted to know when you awoke."

"Wait!"

Paige jerked to a halt. She turned. Thane's eyes were filled with darkness. The grief, the need to cry, was etched in every line of his face. It took everything Paige had not to automatically wrap her arms around him, hold him and let him cry. That was what he needed, she realized. The tears glimmered in his eyes. He looked away, as if ashamed that she'd seen them.

"Yes?"

"Paige…I…hell, I'm feeling pretty upset right now. I'm sorry. I didn't mean to take it out on you."

The forgiving smile that blossomed across her full lips was more than he deserved in the aftermath of his apology, Thane realized as he watched her hungrily. Paige was the only person he knew here. The only person he *wanted* to know. She represented a safe harbor to him, emotionally. The only safe one.

"I'm used to people being in pain and barking like angry dogs, so don't worry about it. Pain makes a person grumpy. Okay?"

Thane ruthlessly looked her up and down. Did she mean it? Or was her response just empty words designed to make him feel better? No, Paige was telling the truth. Thane could see how every emotion she felt could be read in her face. In that way, she hadn't changed much, from what he recalled. She was one

of those people who couldn't hide her true feelings.
Even now, she didn't try to. Thane marveled at that.
Life had taught him to hide beneath a mask most of
the time.

"Okay," he said, his voice raspy with emotion.
"You're the only friend I've got here. I don't want
to chase you away by being a grump."

Touched, Paige felt her lips curve deeply. "I'm
honored to be considered your friend." And she was.
Johnny had said no one would ever want her—not
even as a friend. Maybe he was wrong? Her heart
rose with hope.

Thane knew that the Navajo valued friendship a
lot more than most people. Being considered a friend
was like being adopted into the family. He managed
a broken smile. "From what I understand, you're going to have to put up with me when I get out of this
place, until I can get back on my feet."

She placed her damp, cool hand on the doorknob.
"Yes. You're stuck with me, I'm afraid. Judy has
fixed up the guest bedroom for me to stay in. I work
part-time over at her house, anyway. She's so busy
with the ranch that she needs me to take care of the
house for her on weekends." She didn't add that
Judy needed the help and couldn't afford a cowhand.
Because Judy had been tireless in her efforts to help
the Navajo poor, this was Paige's way of thanking
the woman for her generosity toward Paige's people.

How much Paige wanted to stay and just talk to
Thane. To catch up on his life. In her heart, she was
sure he had a woman whom he loved and who loved
him fiercely in return. He didn't wear a wedding ring,
and Judy Hamilton had never said Thane was mar-

ried, but Paige couldn't imagine him not having a woman who loved him.

Thane scowled at the mention of his mother. "I'm sure she's glad you're there," he managed to murmur as he struggled with an array of dark emotions.

Paige tilted her head. Thane's face had closed once more when she'd mentioned his mother. Sensing something was wrong, but not quite knowing what, she whispered, "I'll call your mom. And I'll tell Dr. Briggs to drop by and see you. I know he wants to do everything he can to save your leg. He and Mr. Trayhern had a long talk about you." Forcing a smile she didn't feel, Paige added, "There's more things for you to consider, but you look tired and I know you're feeling a lot of grief right now."

"Wait...."

Paige hesitated halfway through the opened door. She heard the desperation in his voice.

Thane gulped. She stood like a beautifully poised deer, one hand on the door and the other on the jamb. "You'll be back, won't you?"

Touched, she laughed gently. "Of course. I have a double assignment with you. Mr. Trayhern has asked Dr. Briggs to allow me not only to be your R.N. while you're here at the hospital, but also to be your masseuse. I said I would." She'd jumped at the opportunity, but Paige would never tell Thane that. He had no idea of how she felt toward him.

Relieved, he lay back. "Good...good..."

"I'll see you in a little while," she promised.

The door closed. Thane released a trembling sigh. He looked at his leg, which was again raised slightly. The position stopped blood clots from forming and killing him. Though he was assured he was in good care, he wanted to view his leg. To see what it really looked like. But it was swathed in layer upon layer of white bandages. The number of sterile white dressings attested to the seriousness of his injury, Thane knew.

Sighing, he moved his hand nervously along the blankets on his right thigh. His mother was coming. How the hell could he steel his heart, his emotions, against her? For six years he'd felt imprisoned by her. He resented what she'd done to him by divorcing his father. It had felt like incredible freedom to leave her ranch after his graduation from high school. Thane had never looked back. The most he would do was send her a card at Christmas and her birthday, out of social obligation.

Lifting the glass of water, he sipped it thirstily. How was he going to deal with his mother? Would she fuss over him? Want to hug him? Cry? Thane disliked all those possibilities. He didn't *want* her compassion. He didn't want anything from Judy Hamilton. Grimly, his mouth flexing, he glared at the door. Reminding himself of his focus—saving his leg—he forced himself to accept the fact that he had to stay at the ranch house with her. His mind could make the transition; his emotions were another story.

"Knock, knock. Thane?"

Jerking his head up, Thane heard his mother's strong, firm voice. He frowned. The door opened, revealing a woman who was almost six feet tall, wearing a long-sleeved white blouse, blue jeans and cowboy boots. Her dark brown hair was streaked with silver at the temples.

"Come in," he snapped. Anger edged his voice, though Thane tried to control it. It was old resentment from his teenage years. He'd thought that with time it would go away. But it hadn't; it was right here, palpable, aching to be released. Clamping his lips together, Thane watched as his mother entered the room.

He was shocked by how much she'd aged since he'd seen her two years ago at his father's funeral. There was a faded beauty to Judy Hamilton. She had always been a tall, noble-looking woman with an attractive oval face, strong chin and broad cheekbones. Her green eyes, so like his own, were large and clear. There were fine lines around the corners of her eyes and smiling mouth, and the silver strands at her temples gave her an air of authority. In one hand, she held a bouquet of yellow roses. In the other, an old, dusty, black felt Stetson. The hat, combined with the black leather belt with a large silver oval buckle she wore, made her look like a cowboy.

He saw the sparkling warmth in her eyes as she cast him a quick glance, yet she hesitated for a moment in the doorway and he saw a perceptible tremble in her long, worn fingers. She was nervous. Well, why shouldn't she be? he asked himself angrily. Flexing his hands into fists, Thane watched her approach. His mother had always been a supreme athlete. The years of running a cattle ranch had done nothing to lessen her proud stature. There wasn't an ounce of fat on her body. She still had those same straight shoulders and long legs. Her skin had been sun-darkened by her years of hard, outdoor work.

The smile on her face was one of genuine welcome. Thane felt badly over that. He didn't wish to inflict pain on his mother—he just didn't want her in his life, that was all.

"Hi, stranger," she said warmly as she came over to his bedside. "It's good to see you, Thane."

He steeled himself. Was she going to lean down and kiss him on the cheek? The last thing he wanted was physical contact of any kind with her.

"How are you, Judy?"

She hesitated at the coldness of his greeting. Seeing the glitter in his eyes, that frosty anger that he still obviously felt for her, she nervously waved one hand. "Oh, I keep busy, Son. Believe me. Look, I brought you some roses from my garden. I thought you might want something of Mother Nature near you." Looking around, she murmured, "I hate hospitals." She gave him a sad-eyed look as she picked up an empty vase from the shelf near the bed. Placing the vase on the bedstand, she took the pitcher and filled it with water. Having something to do helped ease her nervousness.

Thane looked at the roses, which were bright and huge. "I didn't know you had a thing for flowers."

Ignoring the sarcasm in his voice, she deftly placed the half-dozen roses into the vase. "I love all things that grow." Smiling gently, she set them near the window. "Looks like your friends are very thoughtful, too." She leaned over a huge bouquet of red, pink and white Oriental lilies and smelled them. "Mmm...wonderful fragrance." Lifting her head, she turned, keeping the smile on her face. "I'm sure it's preferable to the hospital smells around here."

Thane nodded slightly. The tension in his body was obvious. He hated himself for the way he was treating her. Why couldn't he be more civil? He wished Paige were here instead. She calmed him, soothed the restless, biting, snarling beast within him. Judy only exacerbated all his raw feelings.

Coming back to the bed, Judy clasped her hands in front of her. It was obvious Thane did not want to be touched by her. That hurt. Badly. Judy tried to understand the source of his anger—the fact that she had torn him away from the father he worshipped like an idol. Thane had never understood why she'd left Colin. And he'd never asked why, either. She had hoped that, with time and maturity, they could talk about those life-altering events. But Thane had stubbornly championed his father against her at all costs. She was the enemy—still. Sadness touched her and she wanted to cry. But tears would only harden Thane's position against her, she knew.

Placing her hands on the rail of his bed, she said in a cheery tone, "Paige and I were thrilled you could come here to recuperate. I was so glad Mr. Trayhern called me and told me what was going on and—" her voice dropped "—what happened." Checking the urge to reach out and touch his shoulder, which was raised defensively, Judy whispered, "I'm so sorry for the loss of your men, Thane. I can't even begin to know what you're feeling...."

"No, you can't."

Judy compressed her lips. She saw the hardness of his jawline, that stubbornness he was famous for.

He'd gotten that from his father, not her. Judy prided herself on being flexible. Owning a small cattle ranch, she had to be. Moving her fingers along the cool metal railing, she murmured, "Is there anything I can do for you, Son? For the families of the men who died?"

Heart pounding hard in his chest, Thane could feel himself breathing deeply. He felt savage. He felt raw, having his mother so close to him. "No. Nothing." *Not ever.*

Trying to hide her reaction, she stilled her hand on the railing. "Are you happy that Paige will be taking care of you once you get out of here?"

He nodded. "It's fine."

Tears burned in her eyes. Judy turned away briefly, then, forcing herself to face him again, she looked down at his strong profile. How much he looked like Colin, in every conceivable way. She wanted to cry. She had hoped the way Colin had treated her would not be carried on in Thane, but some of her ex-husband's attitudes had taken hold in her son, from what she could tell. It was like having her ex-husband back all over again. His monosyllable answers. His harshness. His uncaring and abusive way. Drawing in a steadying breath, Judy said, "If you want me to come and visit, you can call me. I'm not going to force myself upon you, Thane. I know how you feel about me. I'm happy to give you a home where you can rest and recuperate. Paige will be working with you, I won't. And if you want something, Paige will be there for you. That way, maybe your stay with me won't be so painful. More than anything, I want to see you well and healthy again.

I know how much the Corps means to you. How much you love it. I'll do everything in my power to help you.''

Thane felt his heart breaking with sadness. He didn't dare look up at his mother. The quavering in her voice tore at him. Her words came out low and with an honesty that scored his smarting conscience.

''The ranch house is a little different from what you remember,'' she continued. ''Your room is at one end of it, mine at the other. The kitchen is in the center, and the living room is near your bedroom. Paige's room is right next to yours. Mr. Trayhern is paying to have a two-way radio system put between your room and Paige's in case you need something at night. He's seen to it that your room has the finest of equipment. The den is being remodeled as we speak, into a physical therapy room where you can get your strength back and learn to walk on that leg when it's time. I hope you've thanked him for his overwhelming generosity. He's one in a million, from where I stand.''

Nodding abruptly, Thane tried to take the ice out of his tone. ''I've already thanked him.'' And then, more huskily, he added, ''I think this arrangement will work out. Thanks for opening your home to me.''

Nodding, Judy lifted her hand from the rail. ''Well, I'd best get going.'' She settled the black cowboy hat on her short, wavy hair. ''It's time to feed my stock and I don't have help anymore, so I can't let grass grow under my feet. I'll see you later, Son. I love you....''

Swallowing hard, Thane looked through his lashes

as his mother moved toward the door and opened it. He wanted to call out, to apologize, but everything jammed up in his throat. Without a backward look, she left.

"You bastard," he muttered out loud. "You didn't have to treat her like that."

What the hell was wrong with him? Thane didn't try to blame it on the fact that he was in trauma, that he'd nearly died or that he'd lost four of his best friends. No, this was something old that had stuck in his gullet since his youth. His mother had treated him as if nothing were wrong. She always had. She, at least, was gracious toward him. Thoughtful as well as generous. But the fact that he wouldn't have to interface with her on a daily basis was a huge load off his tensely drawn shoulders. Paige would take care of him—that he would welcome with open arms. His mother was trying her best to stay out of his way. To remain out of his life—like he wanted it.

Then why the hell did he feel so damned guilty? So bad inside? Rubbing his chest, Thane glared at the door. And then he shifted his gaze to his injured leg. He couldn't lose it. He just couldn't! Maybe when Dr. Briggs came in, he'd give Thane a more hopeful outlook. Maybe...

Chapter Four

"Geez," Nurse Jodie Smith whispered fiercely to Paige, "don't go in there! That marine officer is a real *bear!* He's lopping heads off right and left!"

Paige halted in the hall just outside Thane's room. Jodie, who was short and plump, looked harried, and ran her fingers quickly through her short blond hair, an aggravated look on her face.

"What happened?"

Rolling her eyes, Jodie said, "Dr. Briggs gave him the bad news that he'd probably lose his right leg—eventually. Captain Hamilton was not, to say the least, happy about his prognosis. I mean, who would be? We have sympathy for him. But now Hamilton is snapping off the head of everyone who has to go in there and do anything for him. Martha, the dietitian, just left in tears. He chewed her out. He bullied me, but I shoveled it right back at him. Who does he think he is?'' She blew a strand of hair away from her blue eyes. ''Anyway, lucky you. You're his *private nurse*. I feel sorry for you.'' She started to turn away. ''Oh, I've placed the maggots in his leg wound and they're doing their thing. You might check them in about eight hours. By that time, the little critters oughta have full tummies.''

Paige grinned. Jodie, who was in her fifties, was a ball of fire around the floor. ''Thanks for the warning. I'll put on my armor and lift my shield as I go in there.''

Jodie wrinkled her nose. ''Boy, I feel sorry for you! Word's out you gotta take care of this guy full-time when he leaves here to rehab at his home near Sedona?''

Paige nodded.

Jodie whistled softly. ''Well, you've got my sympathy, kiddo.'' She lifted her hand. ''I'm off! Gotta get down to out-patient surgery to help out a doc. Bye!''

Lifting her own hand, Paige felt her smile fading. She ached for Thane and understood his anger, his lashing out. For a man of action like him, the supreme athlete, a former football player and now an accomplished marine, the possibility of losing his leg was shattering. Turning, her lips compressed, Paige allowed the warm memories of her old crush on Thane, those wonderful euphoric sensations from so long ago, to curl warmly around her heart. Because of her love for him back then, she knew she could armor herself to deflect any anger he might throw at her. Pushing open the door, she went in.

Thane looked distraught as she quietly entered his room. He quickly tried to don an implacable mask as she allowed the door to close behind her.

"I'm here to record your blood pressure and pulse," she said softly as she approached his bed. Let him bring up the diagnosis about his leg, she thought. Paige knew from experience that everyone handled things like this differently. Sometimes letting the patient talk about it on his own was best. She saw Thane fidgeting restlessly with the blankets beneath his hands. His eyes were narrowed and dark with anger. Setting the chart on his lap, she said, "You can help me out by holding that for a moment." She figured if she gave him something to distract himself, it might help. Paige looked at the overhead monitor that constantly recorded his blood pressure.

"My!" she said in a teasing tone. "Your blood pressure is skyrocketing. It's 200 over 100." She felt him tense as she lifted the chart from his hands to record the information.

"Yours would, too, if someone told you that you were gonna lose a leg," he muttered. Despite his tone, he realized just seeing Paige helped take the edge off his anger and his shock. The soft, gentle smile on her mouth was angelic looking. Her thick, black hair shone beneath the fluorescent lights. Every move she made was incredibly graceful. He voraciously absorbed her presence.

"I heard," Paige murmured. Placing the chart back in his lap, she picked up his right wrist and put two fingertips beneath it to locate his pulse point. Looking at her watch, she tried to concentrate on her duties. How often had she wanted to touch Thane when she was a dreamy teenager in high school? Oh, so many times! Paige had fantasized about it at night, in bed. Sometimes she'd dreamed of Thane kissing her. Feeling heat starting to steal up her neck and into her face, Paige compressed her lips. She had to concentrate!

Paige's touch was electric to Thane. Her fingertips were cool. Soothing. Her mere presence threw icy water on the raging emotions he could barely control. Hell, he was still breathing hard. He wanted to cry. But marines didn't cry. And trying to stuff away his fears over losing his leg wasn't working very well, either.

"You heard everything?"

Reluctantly, Paige released his thick, hairy wrist. "Yes, I heard how my friends are running away from your room. You're getting quite a name for yourself." Lifting one corner of her mouth, she looked directly at him, his chart in hand. The mild way she said it didn't rebuke him as much as letting him know he was hurting her friends' feelings.

Scowling, Thane avoided her direct, unexpected look. The old Paige he knew would never have confronted him like this. What did he expect? She'd grown up. She was no longer a frightened little shadow. No, she was a mature young woman. Even though she wore a loose-fitting smock, she couldn't hide her femininity from him.

"I should apologize to them," he muttered under his breath. "Can you...?"

"I'd be happy to," Paige told him lightly. "They're here to help you, not hurt you. And I know it might be hard to believe, but they're just as sad as you are over what Dr. Briggs discussed with you about your leg. So am I.'' She put the chart down and removed the stethoscope from around her neck, stuffing it into the pocket of her smock.

Blowing out a breath of frustration, Thane studied her as she opened up the recently applied dressings and studied his leg critically.

''Well? Do you think Briggs will hack it off?''

Paige tried to keep her expression neutral. Thane's leg was in worse shape than she'd realized. Squelching her fear for his sake, she gently reapplied the dressings and added new roller bandages around them so they would stay in place.

''I don't know. But I do know this, Thane—Dr. Briggs is the *best* at what he does. And I know he knows how important it is to you to keep your leg.''

''Humph. He looks like any other surgeon to me. The only way this guy makes money is to hack off body parts. That's what surgeons get paid to do, isn't it?''

She grinned a little and checked the tension on the pulleys on his leg. ''That's true, but Dr. Briggs is going to make money on you whether you keep the leg or not. He's an international consultant, you know.''

His mouth lifted slightly. ''I like your sense of humor.''

''And I like yours. A little cutting, but we'll survive it.'' Turning, Paige allowed herself the pleasure of simply looking at Thane. He was incredibly handsome, with his square face, short black hair and large, penetrating green eyes. His nose was strong looking and had a bump on it where he'd broken it. In high school, he'd had it broken on at least two occasions she could recall in his battles for the state football title play-offs. What was new was the one-inch scar near his left eye.

"How did you get that scar?" she asked, pointing toward his face.

Thane touched the deep scar with his hand. "That…" He shrugged, as if it meant nothing. "On a mission."

"Oh?" Paige came to his bedside. She shouldn't enjoy his company so much, but she did. All those years of pining away, of fantasizing about having Thane to herself, had suddenly come true. Paige was reeling internally from it, but she wouldn't disallow the delicious feelings bubbling up through her. If Thane knew what she was really feeling, he'd probably throw her out of the room, too, because it was decidedly selfish of her to savor this time with him when the reality was that Thane was facing the possibility of losing his leg—and his career.

"Yeah," he muttered, avoiding her direct gaze, which was soft with compassion, "I got this about a year ago on a mission into Bosnia. We—my team and I—were sent in to rescue an American woman who'd been kidnapped by Serb forces and was being held for ransom. She was the wife of some billionaire who was doing charity work for the Bosnians and the Serbs didn't like it—or her. Of course, if she'd been helping the Serbs instead, it wouldn't have happened."

Fascinated, Paige rested her hip against the bed

and studied his tortured expression. "And did you rescue her?"

He nodded. "Yes. We all got out alive."

"But not without injury?"

Shrugging, he rasped, "I took a rifle butt in the side of my face, compliments of a pissed-off Serb. I wouldn't answer his questions and he knocked me out cold. My teammates intervened seconds later, picked me and the woman up and took off for our landing zone, where a Boeing Apache helo was hightailing it to rescue us. I came to later, on the helo." Rubbing the scar self-consciously, he added, "I got a broken cheekbone out of it, was all. The docs at the military hospital in Germany did what they could. They said unless I wanted plastic surgery, I'd have this scar for the rest of my life." He lifted his head and held her luminous gaze, all his anger dissolving. What kind of magic did Paige possess to chase away his fears and his rage like this? "I don't do plastic surgery. I don't like anyone cutting into me unnecessarily."

"You're a genuine hero, Thane."

He arched emotionally beneath her softly spoken words. The pride in her eyes made him feel good about himself. Suddenly self-conscious, he muttered, "My team was heroic. I was knocked out cold for a quarter of the mission."

Reaching up, she gently moved her fingers lightly across the pale pink scar, shocked by her own audacity. But something in her told her that he *needed* to be touched. It would help calm him and release his fears. As she brushed the old wound, she felt him freeze momentarily. Instantly, she withdrew her fingers. Perhaps he didn't want to be touched by her, after all. Her brows dipped and she took a step back. "I'm sorry...."

"No!" Thane said thickly. "I just wasn't expecting it, was all." And he hadn't been. When he saw the uncertainty in her cinnamon eyes, that old shyness returning, he blurted, "Look, in my business we don't usually have the luxury of a beautiful woman around, to touch and heal us when we're in pain. That's why I tensed. It had nothing to do with you."

Feeling embarrassed by her unexpected boldness, Paige scrambled to cover her strewn feelings. She had found by touching Thane, however briefly, that she only wanted to do it more. Much more. "Oh..." So much for an intelligent comeback. And he had called her beautiful! Her! She wasn't, of course. Johnny had reminded her daily that she was ugly. Still, it was nice that Thane saw her in that way. Her heart skipped a beat.

Thane saw the color of her cheeks deepen and realized she was blushing. Her lashes were down and he couldn't read her eyes. She stood humbly before him, her hands clasped in front of her, her head to one side to avoid his eyes. This was the old Paige he knew from high school. The shy Navajo who would never engage in eye contact with him.

"You mentioned earlier that you're a trained masseuse, too," he murmured, trying to reestablish contact with her. "And Dr. Briggs confirmed that as soon as my leg was healed up enough, you'd be working with me in that capacity."

Clearing her throat nervously, Paige nodded and opened her hands, risking a glance at him. What she saw in his smoky green eyes confounded her. She sensed desire all around him. Desire? For what? Unable to sort it all out, Paige whispered, "Well...yes, Dr. Briggs believes in using every tool, medically speaking, to help a person heal. He talked to me earlier, before you arrived here, and told me that he wanted me to give you a full body massage once a day. I won't be able to touch your right leg for a while, but what the massage will do is stimulate your immune system, which will help to fight the infection you have in the bones of your foot."

"He said the maggots will eat away my dead flesh and create paths for new capillaries, so the blood can get to the tissue and stop the gangrene process. Is that right?"

Paige nodded and gestured toward his right foot. "Yes. You're lucky Dr. Briggs is on your case. Not every doctor thinks maggots are good, but they do help create new blood vessels so that oxygen can be carried by the red blood cells. When that happens, your skin or tissue will live instead of die. And maggots are the fastest way to help create those new capillaries that were destroyed by that rocket blast."

He saw the rose hue subside in Paige's cheeks. Thane had no wish to embarrass her or make her feel unwelcome around him. If nothing else, when she was with him he felt hope. He felt a sense of harmony. He didn't feel this way with anyone else, however. All everyone else managed to do was make him feel even more irritable and growly.

"And the massage? How exactly will that fight the infection?"

She smiled and saw the hope burning in his eyes.

Her heart was still skittering beneath his predatory appraisal of her. And she felt her breasts tingling as his gaze moved to them, and then across the rest of her body. It was a delicious and exciting feeling that Paige had never felt before. She blinked twice and tried to assimilate his question instead of appearing to be a tongue-tied teenager in the presence of his overwhelming masculinity. She realized Thane had no idea of how he, as a man, affected women.

"Massage is designed to increase blood supply, too. It's a wonderful, gentle way to stimulate circulation." She held up her hands. "I love to give my patients a massage. It makes them feel so much better. And touch is so important to healing."

"Is that your Navajo wisdom speaking?"

She shrugged shyly. "Perhaps."

"Isn't your grandmother a medicine woman, as I recall?"

"Yes...she still is. I'm surprised you know anything about me or my family."

It was his turn to smile a little. "Why?"

"Well," Paige murmured, "you were a star football player in high school, always surrounded by girls.... My sisters and I weren't very social. We belonged to no clubs. I'm just surprised you remember anything about us, is all."

Studying her in the quiet room, Thane continued to absorb Paige's calming presence. "And because I was popular, mobbed by girls wanting my attention because I was a sports star, you think I didn't see you?"

Clutching the chart out of nervousness, Paige whispered, "Yes. Exactly. We were nobodies. We were part Navajo and shunned by just about everyone.''

Hearing the pain in her voice, Thane reached out, curving his fingers along her upper arm. As he touched her, he saw Paige's eyes widen enormously with shock. ''Do you know how many times I almost went over to you, to start up a conversation with you, but chickened out because I was afraid to?'' There was wry humor in his voice, but he was very much aware of her—the feel of her firm flesh beneath his fingers. Paige was in terrific athletic shape, and Thane reminded himself that she worked at her family's ranch, as well as being a full-time nurse here at the hospital.

Stunned by the contact of his fingers against her arm, Paige froze. Never had she expected him to touch her! ''Y-you *wanted* to talk to me?'' The words came out in disbelief. A part of her instantly melted beneath his grazing touch. She could feel his male strength, but his gentleness, too. Her heart burst with anguish, with need, and her swiftly beating heart opened like a blossom at his dark perusal and deep, confident tone.

''Yes.'' Thane watched her from half-closed eyes. He *liked* touching Paige. Though he forced himself to release her, he found himself wanting to touch her again. She invited touching and that was disconcerting to him. He'd always seen something mysterious and beautiful about her, but now that she'd ripened into a woman, he felt even bolder about wanting to explore his feelings toward her. Maybe it was his injury. Or his desperation. Thane wasn't sure anymore.

The confusion in her eyes was unmistakable. The parting of her soft, full lips only made him groan internally. She had a mouth made for kissing and worshipping. Thane warned himself that she was probably married or living with a man. Someone as beautiful from the heart outward would not be available, his experience warned him.

Her breath hitched in her chest and she felt a rainbow of emotions running wildly around her heart. "But—why?"

"Why not?"

She stared at him and shook her head. "We were nothing, Thane. We were part Navajo. Our skin color wasn't white like everyone else's, that's why."

Wincing, he whispered, "I know you and other Navajo kids took a lot of verbal insults and teasing from some of the kids at the high school."

"You never did any of those things."

"My prejudice doesn't run in that direction," he murmured, one corner of his mouth lifting in wry amusement. "My prejudice is aimed at my mother."

Paige's brows moved upward. She saw his eyes grow confused. And she heard the pain in his voice. For whatever reason, Thane was opening up to her and revealing something very deep that was bothering him. She tread gently. "I think we all have prejudice. And I'm sure everyone has felt it in one way or another."

"Don't minimize what the kids did to you and your sisters. I saw it, and I didn't like it. You remember how Tommy and his gang used to tease the three of you unmercifully? Pull your hair in class? Make fun of you in the halls?"

Paige rolled her eyes. "Don't even remind me of him and his gang."

"What you don't know is that in the one class you and I took together in our junior year, I saw him yank at your hair. He was sitting directly behind you. And I watched him do it to you day in and day out. You just ignored him. You wouldn't turn around and tell him to stop it. And the teacher ignored the situation, too."

With a sigh, Paige said, "Yes, I remember. I wish I could forget."

"Do you remember the day Tommy stopped pulling your hair and calling you names out in the hallway?"

Raising her eyes, Paige thought for a moment. "Why, yes…he did. I thought the teacher finally told him to stop what he was doing. I was so relieved when that happened. I dreaded going into that class. My stomach would tie into knots. It got so that I'd feel nausea and want to throw up because I was so afraid to go in there and sit in front of him…." Those years came back, and Paige felt an instant emotional reaction.

Thane gave her a savage smile of satisfaction. "That's because Tommy and I had a little 'talk' after school about his hurting you." Thane flexed his fist. "He decided he didn't want to get beaten to a pulp by me, and promised me that he'd leave you and your sisters alone from then on." He saw the surprise in Paige's face, and his smile broadened. "Now you know the rest of the story."

Her lips parted. She was speechless. Thane had protected her and her sisters! And he'd never said a thing to them about it! Why? Confused, she whispered, "But why didn't you tell us? Me? We would have thanked you! We didn't believe anyone liked us...." Obviously, she'd been wrong. How many nights at the ranch had she and her sisters talked about their treatment? Their parents tried to counsel them to just ignore the insults and hurts and to walk with their shoulders back, their heads held high. It had been impossible for them to do that, of course.

Thane lay back and closed his eyes. He was suddenly very tired, but in a good way. Just having Paige around and talking to her was like an automatic release valve for his roiling emotions and fears. "Want to know the truth?" he asked, humor in his tone.

Paige moved closer to his bed. He looked weary. She knew he needed to sleep now that he was off that adrenaline surge he'd received after Dr. Briggs told him the prognosis on his limb. "Yes...I'd very much like to hear the truth."

Her voice feathered across him, much like her fingers had glided softly against the flesh of his cheekbone earlier. If only she would touch him again. An ache filled Thane. It was a sensation he'd never felt before. Or was it? He ruthlessly searched his mind in those seconds. No, that wasn't true...he *had* felt this. And then he laughed to himself. This same ache had filled him every time he saw Paige in high school. She just had a way of easing into his space and awareness that he'd never understood as a teenager. But now, as a man, he was beginning to. It was almost as if they shared a deep affinity.

Narrowing his eyes, his gaze settling on her very serious expression, he said, "Because I was *afraid* to approach you. I felt tongue-tied every time I thought about walking up and talking to you about that—or anything else.'' Laughing derisively, Thane added, ''You intrigued me then, Paige. You were so beautiful, so alone and proud. I knew you took a lot of gibing and taunts at school. I did what I could to stop them when I saw them happen. I guess it was my way of saying that I liked you, but I never got up the courage to let you know how I felt. I was just too scared of you.''

Gripping the tubing on the side of the bed, Paige stared openmouthed at him. The seconds strung between them. Disbelief exploded through her. She couldn't have really heard what Thane just said. She must be making it up. At night, as a teenager, she'd often lain in bed fantasizing about talking to Thane, about the most mundane of things. How he'd react to her, what he'd say…all childish fantasies of a skinny, shy teenage girl who had a terrible crush on the most popular guy at her school.

''You must be kidding,'' she finally exclaimed, her voice hoarse with disbelief.

Opening his eyes more, Thane gave her a lazy smile. ''No, I'm not kidding, Paige. How many times did you see me start to walk toward you and then stop?''

Frantically, she searched her spinning mind. ''Well…several. But I always thought you saw *who* it was and turned away because I wasn't the person you'd been hoping to talk to.''

''Mistaken identification?'' He grinned a little. ''Why is it so hard for you to believe I'd be interested in you?''

"Well...I wasn't popular. I wasn't in any of the cliques or clubs. I was just a shadow in school, trying to get by and survive. I wasn't pretty and I didn't wear the 'in' clothes. That's why."

"What we do to ourselves as kids growing up," Thane murmured gently. He reached out and placed his hand on the side of the bed, palm up. He saw her stare down at his opened hand like it was a snake going to bite her. Did she dislike him that much? Was he offensive looking to her? Maybe she hated military types. Navajo were very peace loving, and war was not in their blood, although the Navajo code-talkers from World War II had helped the marines take the islands in the Pacific.

Drawing in a shaky breath, Paige moved away from his proffered hand. If she reached out and placed her hand in his, she wasn't sure what would happen next. Euphoria swept through her like the sun's heat across a dry, cold winter plain. He liked her! He had wanted to talk to her! Paige didn't kid herself, however. She was sure Thane wanted her as a friend—not a *girl*friend.

"This is all so shocking," she said faintly. "I never knew...never realized...." She gave him a helpless look. The way he was smiling at her gave her more courage. "Your friendship would have been wonderful. I wish I'd known...."

"Paige," Thane said in a teasing tone, "don't ever think that I wanted you merely as a friend. That was part of it. But I really wanted to know *you*, the shy, mysterious, beautiful girl."

More shock bolted through her. Paige took another step back. His hand was still opened. Inviting. She was afraid to touch him. Her mouth going dry, the chart clutched to her breast, Paige could only stand and stare stupidly at him. She saw the warmth in his forest-green eyes…and that look smoldering in them once again. Shaken, she realized it was desire—for her. Impossible! Instantly, Paige rejected that thought and the feelings it aroused.

"Listen," she stammered, "I have other rounds to make. I—I'll be back tonight, just before I go off duty, to check and see how you're doing. I have to go…." And she turned on her heel and raced for the door. Without even looking back, Paige left. Outside, she slumped against the wall and closed her eyes. Her heart was pounding like a trapped rabbit's would. Well, didn't she feel cornered? Trapped?

"Oh, you poor thing!" Jodie whispered sympathetically as she met her in the hallway. She put a hand on Paige's shoulder. "He got you, too, didn't he?"

"What? Oh no…no, he's fine now." Paige quickly stood up and fumbled with her stethoscope.

Jodie gave her a confused look. "You're pale, Paige. You look like somebody whacked you alongside the head with a two-by-four."

Managing a short, explosive laugh, Paige rolled her eyes. "Well, you're right. I've been whacked. But it wasn't what you think, Jodie. I'm fine. Really. I gotta get on my rounds…."

"Okay," Jodie said, her hands planted on her hips, "I just wanted to make sure. Because if Captain Hamilton thinks he can keep abusing the staff, I'm going to tell Dr. Briggs to jump on his case."

Smiling brokenly, Paige waved and rushed down

the hall. "No, he's fine now…civil…so don't tell Dr. Briggs anything."

"Okay…" she called, relief in her voice.

Breathlessly, Paige rushed to the next room, where she had to check the vitals on Mrs. Cornelia Stockton. Paige's heart was pounding and surging with stunned emotions, sudden hope and anxiety. Thane *liked* her. He'd wanted to have a relationship with her. Her! Of all people at the high school, he'd wanted to know her—and not just as a friend. As a girlfriend.

Swallowing hard, Paige could barely contain herself as she entered Mrs. Stockton's room. Somehow she must concentrate on the present, not so many years ago. Yet the man of her dreams, the one she'd ached to have in her arms, to kiss and to love— because she'd loved him so artlessly in high school— was just down the hall from her. How badly Paige wanted to go back and simply sit and talk to Thane, to hear what else she didn't know from him about how he'd felt about her back then. The prospect was daunting. Scary. Elevating. Paige couldn't recall feeling like this since her teen years. And the irony of it was the same man was causing her to feel this way now. What was she going to do? How could she shield him from feelings that still lived and thrived within her, and remain a professional? How? Thane needed her as a nurse now—not a woman. She owed it to him to be there for him, to help him heal. That was all.

Chapter Five

"Hey, Paige! Come over here for a sec," silver-haired Lydia called from the nurses' desk.

Paige stopped her progress toward the hall where she was going to start her rounds. Lydia, a short, wiry woman who wore gold wire-rimmed bifocals on the tip of her nose, was the nursing supervisor for the coming day shift.

"Yes?"

She waved for Paige to come and talk to her at the central nursing station, which was a beehive of activity. Registered nurses in colorful smocks hovered around the bright yellow station like humming-birds dipping for nectar.

Paige detoured, putting her stethoscope around her neck. The floor was busy this morning; a lot of new patients had arrived overnight, some requiring immediate surgery. Post-op floor was her assigned job and Paige always found it interesting; she thrived on the tense atmosphere where everyone needed her immediate help and care. It left little time for boredom, that was for sure. She halted at the desk, resting her arms on the counter. "Yes?"

"It's your patient, Captain Hamilton," Lydia said, frowning.

Her heart thudded. "What's wrong?" Paige asked, unable to hide the fear in her voice.

Lydia quickly looked through several patient files that lay in front of her on the desk. "He had a really *bad* night, FYI. The night nursing super left me a note this morning on his board." She placed the paper with the scribble on it in front of Paige. "Seems like PTSD—post traumatic stress disorder—to me. Does it to you?"

Paige rapidly read the note. "He woke up screaming four times?"

"Yeah. And he refused a sleeping pill. Dumb, if you asked me, but it's his choice."

"He just came off a terrible mission where his entire team was killed," she murmured, her heart aching for him.

"He's traumatized, no question about that. Look, try and persuade him to take a sleeping pill tonight, okay? The man has *got* to get his sleep. He needs everything going for him if he's gonna keep that leg. And losing sleep is going to lower his immune system function and that bone infection will stay. Put it into those terms for him and maybe he'll be a little less harsh about the 'no drugs' end of this deal, okay?"

Nodding, Paige said, "I'll see what I can do."

Lydia's head popped up. "Hey, watch it. He's ten times worse today than he was yesterday. Jodie just got nailed by him when she took his meds in. He's *not* in a good mood. Forewarned is forearmed." She grinned a little. "He was asking for you."

"Me?"

"Why look so stunned?" Lydia's smile increased. "Beauty and the Beast, if you ask me. When you're around, he's actually nice to everyone. When you're not, he's on the warpath. Get in there and calm the savage beast, will you? Have pity on the rest of us." And she chuckled.

"Thanks," Paige said, and she rapidly left the station. As she hurried down the hall, her thoughts moved back to the evening before. She'd stopped out at the Bar H ranch and given Judy Hamilton a report on Thane's progress. Judy was more than grateful to have the updated information. Why wouldn't Thane call her? Paige wondered. She knew Judy was anxious to hear from him. Paige also knew it was none of her business, yet in her heart she knew they desperately needed one another, especially now. Thane was trying to tough it out on his own, and no one with an injury like this, one that threatened an entire way of life and career, ever made it through it alone. No one.

Opening the door, she stepped into the room. Thane was sitting propped up, glaring off into space. He hadn't shaved, the shadow of beard giving his impassive face a dangerous look. His hair was uncombed and tousled. The bedding was messy, the corner at the bottom torn out. His fists were wrapped in the bedspread. When she entered, he snapped his head in her direction. The look of grief she saw in his bloodshot eyes made her draw in a sharp breath.

Undeterred, Paige strode forward. As she did, she noticed his eyes quickly change. Gone was the anger, replaced with hope. Did she have *that* much influence over him? After yesterday's admissions, she had lain awake half the night thinking about what he'd said.

"Hi," she greeted him in a sunny voice. "I hear you had a rough night?" She set the chart down on the bedstand and lifted a pen from the left breast pocket of her bright apple-green smock. As she had dressed today, she'd felt more festive than usual and had put velvet ribbons in various shades of green in her hair after she'd fashioned it into a ponytail. Dainty greenish-blue turquoise earrings completed her accessories. Even though nurses had to wear standard clothing in a hospital, Paige liked dressing in bright, cheery colors, and she loved wearing earrings and small necklaces that enhanced that effect for her usually depressed or hurting patients.

Thane felt like a starving wolf, dying for her attention, her presence. He'd never been so glad to see anyone as he was to see Paige this morning. Releasing his iron grip on the bedclothes, he growled, "Yeah, bad. I'm sure you heard all about it out there. No one else will venture close to my room this morning." He watched every graceful move she made as she logged his blood pressure from the monitor over the bed. He waited for her to take his pulse. He desperately needed her soothing touch.

"I'm sorry," Paige whispered gently. "They said

you were screaming last night.'' Picking up his wrist, she saw him sigh and watched as the tension began to bleed out of him. Maybe Lydia was right. Maybe her touch *was* healing and calming to him. Paige's heart soared with the knowledge as she watched Thane allow his head to ease back on the pillows, his lashes drop. She had difficulty paying attention to the second hand of her watch. Feeling the taut texture of his wrist, the latent power of his muscles, she felt her heart begin skipping beats again. Funny, when she was a teenager and he'd glanced in her direction, her heart had done the same thing. Some reactions, Paige decided, never changed with time. She smiled inwardly.

''Tell the nursing staff I'm sorry, will you?''

His voice was rough. She heard the unshed tears lodged in his throat. He swallowed and his Adam's apple bobbed several times. ''I will,'' she soothed. ''They understand, Thane. They don't take it personally.''

The wild, rampant grief was striking him hard now. He fought back the hot, pricking tears that tried to deluge his eyes. Swallowing several times, he spoke, his voice low and unsteady. ''Every time I shut my damned eyes, I saw them. My men…I saw each of them dying. It was—''

Paige placed his hand back on his lap. After recording the reading, she set the chart aside. ''I know what you need,'' she said softly. Moving to the bathroom, she drew out a bottle of oil and brought it back to his bedside. He had opened his eyes and was watching her hungrily. ''I'm going to give you a minimassage, starting with your face, neck, shoulders and arms. Dr. Briggs has already approved a full body massage for you. Right now, I think you need a little T.L.C.'' She smiled and tilted her head. ''Are you game?''

Was he? Paige was going to touch him. He was desperate for her touch to soothe his raw, burning emotions. Choking back a sob, he nodded abruptly. He didn't dare speak for fear he'd burst into tears. Closing his eyes, he lay back and waited.

''Ever gotten a massage before?'' Paige asked, uncapping the bottle of scented almond oil.

Thane shook his head, afraid to speak. His heart hammered in anticipation of her touch.

Paige felt her heart racing. She *wanted* to do this for Thane. Her heart was crying out in pain for him because she saw the tears in his eyes. More than anything, he needed a little care, a little holding and nurturing. She could at least give him that much from a professional standpoint. Pouring oil into her palm, she moved closer, her body pressed against the railing as she reached up and began to smooth her fingers across his tense and wrinkled brow.

The instant Paige's fingers glided across his forehead, Thane released a ragged sigh from his tightly compressed lips. Paige was so close. He could feel the heat of her body as she leaned over him. Nostrils flaring, he caught the scent of sage around her. It was a good, clean smell. The smell of the outdoors, where he so desperately wanted to be right now. He hated being cooped up. He hated this prison of a hospital room.

He absorbed each light, coaxing stroke like a man thirsting for water. Her fingers glided from the center of his brow to his temples and then back again. So much of the tension he held inside of him began to miraculously evaporate as she continued her gentle assault across his nose, his cheekbones and then down along his tightly clenched jaw. His skin tingled. He felt like a thief, stealing energy from her, stealing whatever she would share with him. Right now, he felt so empty, and somehow she was filling him with her quietness, her calmness and serenity, when he had no peace himself.

Paige tried to steady her heart. Oh, to be able to touch Thane like this! It was a dream come true for her. She tried to balance her selfish reaction to the pleasure of moving her fingers in light, gliding motions across his hard, anxious-looking face. With each stroke, she saw and felt him release a little more of that internal, explosive tension that had been eating him alive since she'd entered the room. With each smoothing movement, a little more stress bled away beneath her fingertips. Within five minutes, his face was devoid of strain and tightness. Even his lips parted beneath her cajoling movements. Smiling to herself, Paige felt euphoric. It was a small gift to give Thane.

To her surprise, as she worked on releasing the tension in his thick, corded neck, he fell asleep. Pleased, she kept her strokes light. She could feel the knots in his taut flesh, all from the rocket attack that had nearly killed him. Paige was sure that the force of the attack had flung him through the air and he'd landed on a hard, unforgiving surface, because the right side of his neck and shoulder were like a resistant rock of muscle beneath her fingers. The body always remembered. And that was one of the many gifts of massage: she could, with daily work, begin to get his body to release and eventually forget the trauma.

Looking down, she saw he was sleeping deeply, his lips slightly parted, his breathing slow and heavy. *Good.* What he needed more than anything was deep, healing sleep. She continued to work on the exposed areas of his neck and shoulder, but did not remove the light blue pajama top. It was short-sleeved, so she focused on his right arm and then his left, using gentle, kneading strokes to continue to assess his condition. Compared to his knotted up right side, Thane's left side was more supple, more giving beneath her coaxing fingers, confirming her belief that he'd landed hard on his right side.

When she was done, Paige wiped her hands on a nearby towel. Above all, she wanted Thane to sleep. She would tell Dr. Briggs to drop by on his afternoon rounds, and she'd place a Do Not Disturb sign on Thane's door so that the nurses would leave him alone. Because he'd been so cranky to the staff earlier, Paige knew they'd be more than happy to do so.

Hesitating, she looked out the window. It was a bright sunny day in Sedona. The yellow flowers near the corner of the window were startling and beautiful. All colors seemed more vibrant here in the Southwest.

Looking down at Thane, she felt a little guilty because now she could simply absorb him into her being without him being aware of it. Reaching out in an act of pure spontaneity, she ran her fingers through his short, mussed hair and smoothed it into a semblance of order. At this moment he looked like a hurt little boy. How much she wanted to lean over, slide her arms around him and just hold him. That was what he really needed—holding and rocking.

Gone was all the rage, the grief and tension that had marked his face before. Paige was more than grateful that she knew massage as an adjunct to being an R.N. It came in so handy sometimes. As she lifted her fingers from his dark, thick hair, she hesitated fractionally. Oh, to lean over and kiss those strong lips of his!

The idea was shocking. Hot. Provocative. Paige instantly jerked her hand away and quickly turned on her heel. What was wrong with her? Touching her own lips with her fingertips, she closed her eyes and halted at the door. She felt warm and weak all over. There was a gnawing ache in her lower body. A yearning. Opening her eyes, she took in a deep, ragged breath. Somehow, over the years, she had never lost the love for Thane that had taken root in her when they were in high school. How could that be? Paige quietly opened the door and slipped out of the room.

Hurrying to the nurses' station, Paige busied herself relentlessly. Somehow she had to purge herself of these wild, unbidden feelings toward Thane. He didn't love her—but she loved him. It was disconcerting and shocking that all these emotions were now erupting through her like an uncontrolled explosion from an inner volcano.

No matter what she did the rest of that morning, Paige could not escape her emotions. At noon, while eating in the hospital cafeteria with her friends, Jodie and Lydia, she felt helpless and she didn't feel comfortable sharing her unexpected feelings with her two co-workers. Maybe tonight she could talk to her sisters; but they were so busy trying to keep their sheep ranch afloat that she rarely saw them until they dragged in around midnight before a late supper before falling into bed, exhausted from the day's demands.

Forcing herself to eat, even though she had no appetite, Paige looked forward to going with Dr. Briggs this afternoon to see how Thane's injury was coming along. She more than hoped that the surgeon would see progress.

Thane held his breath. Dr. Briggs, with Paige's help, was cleaning off his leg. Thane had slept deeply until the doctor had come in at 3:00 p.m. to check the progress of his wound. The badly needed sleep put Thane in a better mood. Paige had given him a small smile of welcome when she walked in with Briggs moments earlier. Thane still needed to thank her for what she'd done for him. Her touch was miraculous.

"Well?" he demanded. "What do you see? Is it better?"

Briggs, a man in his fifties, lean as a whippet, with dark-framed glasses perched on the end of his beak-like nose, looked up momentarily. "The maggots are helping to create better circulation down here, Captain Hamilton. That's the good news."

Restlessly Thane watched as Paige continued to clean off his ugly looking red and swollen leg. He felt little pain, thanks to the medication dripping from the IV into his bloodstream. Today he could feel her touching him, and that was a good sign, because yesterday the limb had felt numb.

"What's the bad news, then?"

Briggs handed over the cleaning and dressing job to Paige, then picked up his chart and put some notes on it. Looking up again, he said, "I'm worried about bone infection, Captain. It's our biggest problem in any injury like this. I've asked Rachel Donovan-Cunningham, a homeopath, to come over and take your case." He looked at his watch. "She should be arriving here shortly. Nurse Black will explain to you what homeopathy is and how it works before Ms. Donovan-Cunningham arrives. I've found that homeopathy, linked with our traditional procedures to cure bone infection, gives you the best chance of recovery." He smiled a little. "And no bone infection means you keep your limb, Captain, so I suggest you work with Ms. Donovan-Cunningham. Even if you don't believe in alternative medicine, I do. I don't have to amputate, in many cases, because of its efficacy."

"Okay," Thane said, "I'll do it. Then what? What are you looking for?"

"In the next two weeks, with continued antibiotic and homeopathic treatment, we should see all the infection go away. If it does, then Dr. Jennifer Logan, our physical therapist, will begin putting you on a very painful regime to get your muscles back into shape and help you stand and then walk on that limb. Right now, though," he warned, pushing the glasses up on his nose, "expect to be in bed or a wheelchair to get around. You've got a lot of bones that need this time to heal up properly.''

''When can I start walking?''

Briggs smiled slightly. ''Don't be in a hurry, Captain. You're looking at a *year,* minimum, before you can even think of walking normally again.''

Shocked, Thane rasped, ''A year? You've got to be kidding me! I need to get back to my job. I'm a marine. A Recon. I want to get back to my unit—''

''Whoa, Captain,'' Briggs warned, holding his hand up, ''let's downsize your grandiose plans, shall we? *If* we can eradicate the infection here, you need a minimum of six to eight weeks for those bones to heal up before you can put any weight at all on that ankle and foot. Muscles, when they aren't used, atrophy. They must be brought back with hard, repetitive exercise. You're a big man—six foot four, and two-hundred and twenty pounds. That's a lot of weight to put on a foot that was basically in shreds from the injury you sustained.''

A year. Thane's heart sank. Glaring at the surgeon, he snarled, ''It won't be a year. I'll work hard. I'm used to being brutal on my body and demanding things from it.''

Briggs nodded patiently. ''You're young, Captain, that's true. You're lucky to even have that foot attached to your leg at this point. The surgeon down in Cusco did a helluva job reattaching everything. You're looking at at least two more operations to continue to repair the damage and loss of muscles and tissue down there to make your foot work like it should.'' He held Thane's glare. ''You aren't going anywhere in a hurry, Captain, so if I were you, I'd set my attitude for the long haul and not the short run. Okay?''

Compressing his lips, Thane looked away. He saw the compassionate look on Paige's face. *Damn! A year!* A whole year out of his life. He gripped the bedcovers to stop from bursting out like a ten-year-old having a temper tantrum.

''I'm not used to obstacles like this,'' Thane said to the doctor through gritted teeth.

Briggs patted him gently on the shoulder. ''I know, Son. I know. You're a gung ho marine. You're used to punishing your body, ignoring it and doing what has to be done. In this case, you can't do that. You can't and still expect to walk again.''

''Can you promise me I'll be able to do what I did before?'' he asked tightly.

Briggs shook his head. ''No...I can't. You're lucky to have the foot, Captain. That's what I'm trying to get through your head. Even if you can walk on it, that doesn't guarantee you can punish it like you did before and continue being a Recon Marine. There's a big 'I don't know' in this equation. Only time will tell. That and working closely with your physical therapist.'' Briggs hooked a thumb in Paige's direction. ''And getting daily massage to increase circulation and move the lymph fluid down in that area will all work for you, not against you.''

Helplessly, Thane whispered off-key, ''I thought—I thought—well, maybe a couple of months...three at the most...and I could be back with my unit....''

''I'm sorry, Son. It doesn't work like that. I wish it did, but it doesn't.'' Mustering a smile, the doctor gripped Thane's arm for a moment. "But take heart. You've got the best bone team in the States right here. And we'll work with you all the way. We want to see you be all you can be, too. Just be patient with yourself, with your progress, because it's going to be slow. No overnight wonders on this mission, okay?"

As the words sank in Thane felt like crying out in frustration. Paige was watching him now and again as she finished cleaning his leg and reapplying the maggots. He saw the sadness in her eyes for him. Somehow, it took the edge off his grief and shock. "Yes, sir," he muttered. "I'll try to recalibrate my attitude."

"That's it," Briggs said optimistically. "Nurse Black will finish up here. I'll see you tomorrow morning."

Glumly, Thane watched as the doctor left.

"I guess no one told you how bad your injury was," she said.

"No," he sighed. Putting his arms behind his head, he rested against the pillows.

"You love the Marine Corps, don't you?"

"Very much."

"Does it give you everything you want?" she asked, placing the dressings over his leg and taping them lightly over the wound.

"Everything. It's my world. My life. I was born and bred for what I do there."

Paige chewed on her lower lip and avoided his glittering green gaze as she worked on his leg. So much for her fantasy of him wanting to stay here and live. Her heart was so idealistic, so crazy!

"What if your leg doesn't recover enough for the Marine Corps to let you stay in?"

His gut contracted. Easing his arms from behind his head, Thane looked around the room. He felt suffocated. Scared. "You always ask the right questions?"

Paige smiled a little and began to put the extra dressings and roller bandages away. "I'd sure be asking myself the same question."

"I won't even let that be a possibility," Thane said in a dark tone. "I *will* recover. I *will* go back to the Corps. It's where I belong. My dad was a marine general. I want to follow in his footsteps."

Paige nodded and took the protective gloves off, dropping them in a biohazard wastebasket near the door. "Have you ever thought that your mother needs help running the ranch here?"

Thane stared at her. The question took him by surprise. "What?"

She halted near the bathroom. "Your mother runs a cattle spread of nearly a thousand head of beef. She's fifty-eight years old and she doesn't have the money for a hired hand. She's been doing it alone for years, and she's getting old. Judy can't keep up the hours that the ranch demands. I was just wondering, if you couldn't go back to the Marine Corps, whether you might think of staying here and helping her run the ranch."

Paige might as well have dropped hot coals into his leg wound. He glared at her. The desire to snap angrily at her flooded him, but as he ruthlessly gauged the expression on her face, he realized she wasn't saying it to hurt him. No, there was a seriousness in her eyes, and in her low, steady voice. Swallowing his anger, his acidic reply, he hesitated and reordered his thoughts.

"The ranch was *her* idea, not mine. I never had the dream of being a rancher. All I wanted was to be with my father, and she made that impossible. As a kid, I had no rights, and the judge awarded me to her, not my dad. I hated being here. I hated ranching."

"But…you helped her run the ranch when you were here before…."

"Because I *had* to, Paige." Anger boiled up anew. "You work for her. Hasn't she told you this stuff?"

Shrugging, Paige shook her head. "I work two times a week as her housekeeper, is all." Because of the bad feelings he had toward his mother, she didn't want him to know how close she had come to Judy over the years.

Seeing the confusion on Paige's face, he snarled, "My mother decided to up and divorce my father one day. She said it was for my own good, that I needed a stable place to grow up. She wanted to stop moving from base to base, country to country, is what she told me. I loved being with my dad. We were tight. I didn't want to go with her. I thought her reasons were stupid. I was doing fine in every school I went to. My grades didn't suffer because I had to move every two years."

The anger reverberated around the room. Blinking, Paige said, "Thane…I don't think you know the whole story…about your mother and your dad. I mean—"

He nailed her with a dark look. "And I suppose

she confided in you the *real* reason she left my dad and forced me to live here with her?''

Paige went into the bathroom and washed her hands. When she came out, she walked over to his bedside, placing her hands on the cool metal railing. This time she looked him fearlessly in the eye. ''It's not my place to be discussing this with you. I really think you need to talk to your mother in depth about it. From what she's said, you don't know the real reasons why she left your father. And I feel you're judging her harshly because you don't know the truth. I don't know much more than that. Judy never confided details to me.''

Edgy, Thane felt the anger rising in him yet again. ''Look, I don't want to rip your head off because of *her*. Don't defend her, Paige.''

''I'm not defending her, Thane. But you asked, and I'm being honest with you. I've worked for Judy ever since you left Sedona for Annapolis. She's one of the kindest, most giving people I know. I don't feel she deserves your anger. I noticed you haven't called her yet to let her know how you are. Is that any way to treat her? She's so worried about you. I saw her last night and I caught her crying.''

Giving her a sharp glance he snarled, ''Crying?''

''Yes—for you,'' Paige stated firmly. She saw the anger and surprise flare in his eyes. ''She's still in shock over the fact that you could have died.... She loves you so much, Thane. You should see the photos of you in her home. She talks to everyone about you, how proud she is of you being a marine, and being such a hero for people who need your help. She's your greatest admirer.''

Stunned, he stared at her as the silence thickened around them. Guilt struck him fully. "I—I didn't know that."

"And every Christmas, when you send her a card, she is so happy. She always shows them to me and anyone else who comes for a visit to her ranch. She has framed every one of them."

"What?"

Paige tried to be patient with him. His mouth worked and then became a thin line, and she could feel him fighting inwardly against her words. "Judy was never one to complain about how little she heard from you over the years since you left. But each Christmas card was like the greatest gift in the world."

"All I did was send the damn thing...."

"And you never wrote a note."

Thane felt her eyes on him and avoided her gaze altogether. "I don't have to apologize for how I treat her."

Fingers tightening around the railing, Paige found her own anger stirring. "She is your *mother,* Thane. She's not somebody you can just throw away and ignore because of some past hurt or decision she made on your behalf."

"Look, I know Navajo value relatives and are close to everyone in their family," he said through gritted teeth, giving her a look that would wither most people. But not Paige. He saw her standing tall, her eyes flashing with gold lightning, her mouth pursed. It needled him that Judy was crying—for him. Thane wanted to deny that comment. He wanted to be done with his mother once and for all, but that wasn't going to happen.

"Judy Hamilton is a respected member of Sedona. She is a kind woman, a generous woman," Paige told him in no uncertain terms. "She works hard. And she's alone. I know that she's sent you birthday and Christmas boxes every year without fail, and yet, as far as I know, you've never sent her a thank-you note or letter for her care or consideration of you. She loves you, Thane. She's so happy you're here. I saw her perk up when she learned you were coming home to recuperate. I've never seen her as happy as she is now. Please...whatever you think of her, of the past, can't you release it? Can't you start over with her?"

"Dammit, Paige, you're asking too much."

Stepping away from the bed, she looked at the flush staining his cheeks and the stubborn set of his mouth. "This is *not* the Thane Hamilton I know," she quavered. "The darkness in your heart is not the real you. If you could protect me from a gang of boys by confronting them, if you could rescue that senator's daughter in Bolivia, you are a hero. And a hero wouldn't do something like this to anyone— especially his mother!"

Her words rang in his ears. He saw the disappointment in her eyes. Of all people, Thane didn't want Paige to see him as anything less than heroic. Hadn't he spent his life in heroic pursuits? Hadn't he been the man who pulled out all the stops to win the football championship? The marine who risked his and his men's lives to rescue those in need? Now Paige's eyes were filled with disgust. Aimed at him. Her once beautiful lips were flattened. Avoiding her glare, he looked away. How could he convince her he wasn't wrong about his mother?

"You don't understand," he growled.

Paige laughed, her voice a little off-key. "Me? Not understand? Hold on, Thane. I think the shoe is on the other foot here. It's *you* who doesn't understand. You don't know the *real* reason why your mother left your father. You haven't a clue. And yet you're more than willing to swallow whatever was told to you so long ago and believe what you want to believe. Your father wasn't the god you made him out to be, and that's all I'll say. If you want to know the *truth,* then you need to ask Judy."

Fists clenching and unclenching, Thane felt suffocated. He wanted to escape. Of all people, he hadn't expected Paige to turn on him like this—to take his mother's side. Yet his anguished heart told him that Paige wasn't the type of person to rub salt in old wounds for the hell of it. No, she was a fighter for truth. Obviously. So maybe there was something to what she was saying.

"Look," he growled, "when I get transferred home, I'll ask her. But not until then. Right now, I need to conserve my energy and work on keeping my leg."

All the anger drained away from her. Paige nodded. "Okay," she said tremulously, "that's fair enough."

He gave her a glance from beneath his lashes. "So, am I still a hero in your eyes? Or have I turned into a first class bastard instead?"

Shaken, she said unsteadily, "Thane, you were always my hero. Always. And the more I know about you, what you did for me and my sisters in the past, what you've done as a marine to help other people…well, I admire you so much more than ever before. No, you're not a bad person. You're just mixed up, is all. I feel if you talk to your mother, you'll stop blaming her, and maybe then healing can take place between you.''

That was enough. Suddenly spent by the emotional storm within him, Thane sighed and lay back on the pillows. "Heroes have clay feet. Didn't you know?"

Paige walked cautiously to his bedside, reached out and slid her hand into his. "That isn't important," she told him in a low, impassioned voice. "What is important is your heart. You're a good man, Thane. You always have been and always will be. The Navajo look for good hearts, not a two-heart."

A two-heart was a manipulative, selfish person, Thane knew, and he was glad she didn't see him that way. Her hand felt warm and good in his. He curled his fingers around her long, slender ones, an ache centering in his chest. Looking up at her, at all the emotions clearly written across her smooth, lovely features, he managed a tight, one-cornered smile. "I just don't want you to think bad of me, okay? Right now, I need to feel like a hero to someone, even if it's just one person. I'm scared, Paige. I'm afraid of losing my leg…of not being able to go back to the Corps. It's all I know. I don't know *how* to be a cowhand or whatever it is that my mother needs. My life, my heart, is in the military, not here…."

The words cut through Paige. She gripped his hand

and hung her head. "Yes…I understand that. And I know your mother will, too, because more than anything, Thane, she wants you healthy. Your happiness means *everything* to her. She'll support you any way she can to get you back to what you love to do." But even as she said the words, Paige's heart broke. The fantasy of Thane wanting to stay in Sedona, making a home here after he recovered, was shattered. How silly her idealistic heart was, Paige thought as she reluctantly pulled her fingers from his strong, warm hand. Breaking physical contact with him was the last thing she wanted to do, but she had to. She must. Somehow, she had to come to grips with the fact that her love for him would always remain unrequited. Within a year or less, he would be gone from her life—forever.

Chapter Six

"Well, Captain, I've got good news for you," Dr. Briggs said, a wide smile on his narrow face as he stood with Paige at the end of Thane's bed.

Thane's heart pumped hard, underscoring his anticipation of the physician's announcement. He had been in the hospital six weeks and today was the day he was set to leave, pending the results of the tests they'd taken last night to see if the infection was gone. Gripping the railing, he said in a rasping tone, "The lab tests? The infection? Is it gone?" If it was, it meant he could keep his limb. He looked hopefully at Paige. Her cinnamon-brown eyes were sparkling with tears and she was smiling, her lower lip trembling with suppressed emotions.

"You're clean, Son. The infection is gone. You keep your leg." Briggs grinned broadly and, stepping up to the side of the bed, patted Thane on the shoulder. Looking down at Paige, the doctor added, "And as of this moment, you now have a private nurse, twenty-four hours a day, to guide you with your on-going physical therapy. She'll be with you until you can stand on your own two feet again. Nurse Black will accompany you in the ambulance that's waiting to take you home." He thrust out his hand. "Congratulations, Captain. If you'll pardon the pun, you've made a step in the right direction. This next phase is going to be long and hard. And it's going to be painful. The physical therapist will visit you twice a week at your home. I understand from Mrs. Hamilton that two rooms of her home have been re-modeled with everything you'll need to try and get that leg back into shape. And, at a certain point, you'll have that first operation I mentioned. As you heal, I'll do the required surgery to help you progress further."

"That's the best news I've ever gotten, Doctor. Thank you." Gripping the doctor's long, strong hand, Thane felt euphoric. He was going to keep his leg! He saw Paige self-consciously wiping tears from her cheeks. She looked so beautiful to him. So clean. Like a pool of clear water compared to his own murky, muddy emotions, which had plagued him daily these past weeks in the hospital.

Paige gave Thane a wobbly smile of joy as Briggs reached out and clapped him on the back in a con-gratulatory manner. After the doctor left the room, she moved to the side of the bed. The look in Thane's dark green eyes was one of unabashed happiness—

and relief. Reaching out, she touched his broad, strong shoulder.

"Isn't this wonderful?"

Automatically, because he thrived beneath her touch, Thane placed his hand over hers as it rested on his shoulder. She was so close that the wonderful fragrance of fresh sage that always surrounded her filled his nostrils. As he looked up into her flushed features, his gaze settling on those wet, parted lips, the urge to kiss her was overwhelming. During the last six weeks, Thane had drawn emotionally close to her even though he was careful not to broadcast his feelings to Paige. True, she'd been by every day, spending at least an hour or two with him. How he looked forward to the daily massage she gave him. It was like being in heaven, and he was sure that she had healing hands. Not that Thane took credit away from the homeopathic remedy given him, or the aggressive treatment with antibiotics, either. It had all worked to save his leg. And he was more than grateful.

Paige saw Thane's expression change, his eyes turning a smoky, dark green color. She felt his fingers tighten over hers. As he lifted his hand and slid it around her slender neck to draw her down, she was caught off guard. He was going to kiss her! Stunned, she found her lashes automatically closing as she placed her hand on his shoulder and leaned over him. A kiss. Oh, how long she had wanted to kiss Thane! And now it was going to happen.

Paige heard him murmur her name as if it were a prayer. She felt his fingers tighten slightly on the exposed nape of her neck as he eased her face toward his. The hot rush of his breath against her flesh sent wild, untrammeled prickles along her chin and jaw. Never had she wanted anything more than this. Ever. All the years she'd pined for Thane, held that dream of him wanting her as much as she wanted him, melted away. Parting her lips, Paige felt the first tentative brush of his mouth against hers. It was an exploratory touch, full of magic. Filled with tender promise.

With a soft moan, Paige surrendered to him, to his need of her. She was sure he was kissing her in celebration of the good news and nothing more. But as her lips settled with eagerness against his questing mouth, she knew she was kissing him out of the love that had never died within her. All the memories of her hellish, abusive marriage dissolved beneath his coaxing mouth, beneath his gentle exploration of her as a woman. Paige had never been kissed like this, she realized as his other hand moved up to frame her face in a strong, yet incredibly tender, gesture. So unlike her ex-husband, who knew only how to hurt her.

The past slipped away. She lost herself in the splendor of Thane's mouth, the warmth of his ragged breaths, the hunger in his touch, and the power of his need for her. Her fingers dug convulsively into his shoulder. As he kissed her, Thane was at once cajoling and celebratory. The joy he felt sang through her. Paige sipped the heat, the masculinity and the male tenderness he shared with her. Her blood sang through her, the rush of it blotting out every other sound around her. The roughened quality of his fingers against her cheek only heightened her awareness of him. He stroked her flesh as if she were some priceless gift, and it brought a rush of tears to her eyes. Never had Paige felt so incredibly loved as in this moment.

Then, abruptly, panic set in. Paige pulled away, breathing hard. He would leave her. He had already said that as soon as he was able, he'd leave for the Marine Corps. She was not a part of his life and would never be. So how could she risk her heart with him? Could she love him while he was here, and then have the strength to release him when he wanted to leave? *No.* She was a coward. She didn't feel like she had that kind of strength. Her marriage had taken a part of her soul and destroyed it. What was left she could not give to Thane, under the circumstances. Feeling worse than a coward, Paige looked down into predatory green eyes, which held her captive. There was so much she could see in Thane's gaze as he hungrily gazed at her in the golden silence building between them.

Pulling back, she touched her lower lip with her fingertips. "I—I don't know what happened," she whispered unsteadily. "I'm sorry, Thane. We shouldn't have…can't…"

Hurt soared through Thane as he saw the depth of pain in Paige's eyes. The kiss had been beautiful. Achingly beautiful. His mouth tingled in hot remembrance of her soft lips opening to his gentle assault. He knew he hadn't hurt her, and yet distress lingered in her eyes. Why? Confused, he frowned and said, "I'm not sorry, Paige." Hell, he'd been wanting to kiss her since he was a teenager. It was a dream come true for him, but obviously not for her. His conscience nipped at him, at the joy he felt, because she did not share the same feelings. His heart constricted with anguish over that realization. "I won't do it again unless you want me to."

Nodding uncertainly, Paige saw the door to the room open. It was one of the orderlies come to take Thane down to the ambulance. Relief rushed through her. She was grateful for the interruption. Gathering her strewn, boiling feelings, and ignoring the glow of yearning in her lower body, she quickly moved to help the orderly.

Frowning, Thane saw how shaken Paige really was. Her hands trembled as she unhooked the IVs from the apparatus near his bed. Her cheeks were flushed, her eyes bright and languid looking. Dammit, he *knew* she'd enjoyed kissing him. So why did she pull away as if burned? What was the pain in her eyes about? There was a lot he didn't know. Taking a deep breath to steady his pounding heart and get a hold on his desire for her, he told himself he had other obstacles to take care of first.

In the six weeks he'd been at the hospital, he'd not had contact with his mother. He'd promised Paige that once he was at Judy's house, he'd find out more about why she'd divorced his father. Now the time for that confrontation was nearly here. As the orderly lowered the railing to slide him onto a gurney that sat next to his bed, Thane knew that the next few hours were going to be hard ones. He didn't relish talking to his mother. But it had to be done, for a lot of reasons. If, as Paige had hinted weeks ago, there was more to the story than he knew, he owed his mother that much of a courtesy. He owed it to himself. And to Paige, who saw him as a hero, even now when he was powerless and bedridden with a bum leg.

Judy was in her small, Victorian-decorated kitchen when she heard the orderlies bringing Thane in on the gurney through the front door. Her hands trembled as she poured boiling water into a delicate, white china teapot with pink roses hand-painted across it. She thought sharing high tea, her favorite time of the day, with Thane and Paige would be a proper gesture for her son's homecoming.

Trying to steady her nerves, she poured fragrant black tea leaves into a small wire cage assembly, then placed the case into the steaming teapot. Hearing footsteps, she turned.

"Hi." Paige greeted her from the doorway, her hands resting on the jambs. "Don't you look nice!" She saw Judy's oval, lean features grow pink at the compliment.

"Oh," Judy murmured nervously, touching her skirt, "I just thought it would be nice to celebrate. This is a special occasion, you know."

Smiling gently, Paige said, "Judy, I've never seen you in a dress before. Just your Levi's, shirt and cowboy boots." Indeed, today Judy looked as if she'd stepped straight out of the Victorian era. She wore a coffee-colored needle lace chemise gown, with a delicate lace layer over the soft, velvet fabric. The umber lace was highlighted with embroidered gold leaves and flowers across the front panel and down the long sleeves, which reached her thin wrists. The dress hung to her ankles and gave her a decidedly old-fashioned and prim look. Judy loved anything Victorian. Even her house looked as if she had stepped back into the nineteenth century to live.

"Oh, dear...do you think it's too much? Do you think Thane will be—repelled by it?" she asked, her hands moving nervously across the front of the dress.

Paige's heart broke for Judy. Giving her a soft smile of encouragement, she came forward. "I don't think so, Judy. You look beautiful. Like a heroine stepping out of Queen Victoria's realm. I think you look wonderful!" And she did. Today, her hair was carefully coiffed. She wore a black beaded choker with a piece of jet the focal point of the antique look-ing necklace, with eardrops to match.

"I love your jewelry," Paige said. Noticing the tray Judy had set up on the counter, she asked, "So, we're having high tea with Thane? What a great idea." And it was. She knew Judy had been nervous about this meeting for the past week. Although her friend tried to hide her anxiety, Paige knew her too well and could see the nuances that spoke of her concern over her son coming home and living under her roof. Reaching out, Paige ran her hand gently along the woman's tense back. "Relax. It will go fine, Judy. Thane's so deliriously happy about not losing his leg that I think tea and cookies with him will go fine."

"Oh, I hope you're right," she said, placing the teapot on the wooden tray, which was painted with white, pink and red roses. The delicate china cups and saucers trembled as she added them. "I'm just so scared. I'm afraid he'll start yelling at me. Calling me names, like he did when he was growing up."

"Shh," Paige whispered, giving her a hug of reassurance. "He's older now. And more mature. He's a man, not a little boy anymore. I doubt if he'll do that." In her heart, Paige hoped that Thane would treat Judy warmly, and not icily, as he had before. But she wasn't sure what his reaction would be. Right now, he was on top of the world from the news that Dr. Briggs had given him. Perhaps he could find forgiveness in his heart just this one time. She knew he wouldn't realize the pains his mother had taken especially for him, how she had dressed up for his homecoming and prepared tea. Paige hoped Thane would at least be gracious.

Thane had just gotten settled into his new bed, which was exactly like the one in the hospital, when he saw Paige enter with a tray in her hands. She was smiling warmly at him. Right behind her was his mother. He gulped and stared at her. She was dressed in old-fashioned clothing, and looked tall and regal in the outfit. Everything in his bedroom was Victorian, from the furniture to the eggshell-colored curtains, which were crocheted with hanging tassels. Her touch, her love of the past, was everywhere, and oddly, Thane felt himself relaxing because of it. He was home. He'd spent many years of his young life in this room, and it didn't look like it had changed much at all since he'd left.

"Judy thought we'd celebrate your good news by having high tea, Thane. Isn't that wonderful?" Paige placed the tray on the cherry wood bedstand next to his bed. Then she turned and smiled at Judy. "You come pour. This is your celebration, too."

Thane read the anxiety in his mother's eyes. In the dark brown dress, she looked so thin. Her face was worn. As she reached for the teapot, he saw her hand tremble slightly. The china cup clinked several times as she lifted it to pour tea into it. Feeling badly, he knew she was nervous because of him. Of what he might do or say to hurt her. He saw Paige staring pointedly at him, as if to warn him to be nice to her.

"This is nice," he managed to state in a strangled voice, trying his best to sound grateful. It must have worked, because he saw his mother's face relax slightly.

"Tea is so civilized," Judy said as she handed Thane the cup and saucer. "It's the only time of day I come in from my duties around the ranch and just sit and enjoy my break."

"Thanks," Thane murmured as he held the cup in both hands and rested it on his lap.

Paige came forward and accepted her cup. "Judy makes the most wonderful cookies and finger sandwiches. I love to be around when she makes high tea." Paige pointed to a small lazy Susan that had three tiers layered with cookies and sandwiches galore. She brought it over to Thane. Grinning, she said, "Don't be a pig and take them all. Leave a few for us, huh?"

Judy laughed nervously and went to a high-backed chair covered in burgundy velvet. "Paige!"

Thane managed a weak grin and took only a couple of sandwiches. "I'll try not to be a pig."

Paige laughed lightly and took the lazy Susan to Judy next. "Your turn. There's some left. Maybe there's hope for him, after all."

Thane knew Paige was trying to lighten the mood. He watched his mother covertly through his lashes as he lifted his teacup and took a sip. He was nervous, too. And he barely tasted the tea. Paige set the lazy Susan on the dresser and brought up a second high-backed chair so that they both sat near his bed.

A puffy or Pairpoint lamp of apple green with hand-painted pink and red roses on it provided most of the light, and as Thane looked around the dimly lit room he murmured, "The place looks the same."

Judy smiled uncertainly. "Me and this house haven't changed much over the years, Thane. From time to time, I've added more antiques from the Victorian era." She pointed to the large, colorful glass lamp on his dresser. "I found that Pairpoint lamp at a garage sale in Cottonwood, if you can believe it. The woman who sold it to me didn't know what she had…or how much it was really worth. I had electric added to it."

Thane nodded and kept his gaze on the lamp with the tall brass stand. "I remember you liked antiques. What is something like that worth nowadays?"

Heartened that her son was going to be civil to her, Judy breathed with relief. But although she saw Thane struggling to be polite, she didn't take it for granted that his feelings toward her had changed. Still, the fact he was making an effort was more than enough for Judy at the moment. "Well," she said, "if it was signed, it might be worth upwards of twenty thousand or more, but this one isn't signed. I know it's old, but I have no way of verifying it."

"Besides," Paige said, giving him a smile, "Judy collects them because she loves them. Anything old she loves, and over the years, she's been more of a pack rat than anything else.''

Laughing, Judy nodded. ''Guilty as charged. I guess I never throw anything old out. I just hang on to it.''

Thane's conscience nibbled at him. ''I'm old and from your past, and you never threw me out, either.''

Stunned, Judy felt shock, followed by silence, explode throughout the room. Gazing at his sober expression, she didn't see the anger she usually saw in Thane's eyes. Instead, she saw confusion and questioning. She opened her mouth, but didn't know what to say. Was he trying to honestly talk to her? Had he let his guard down? Was he trying to make amends for his past behavior? How much she wanted that to be so!

Resting the cup and saucer on her lap, she looked up and gently held his stare. ''Honey, I would *never* throw you away, no matter what. I love you. That never changes.'' And she forced a smile to hide her nervousness over his possible reaction to her words.

''I guess we need to sit and talk sometime,'' Thane began awkwardly. ''Maybe things from the past weren't as they seemed.'' He looked over at Paige. Her face was filled with compassion, her eyes soft and glowing. He felt her admiration for him. It made him feel good and strong about himself. The look on his mother's face stunned him. She had been so tense and nervous in his presence. Now her face had gone soft, and hope burned in her eyes as she stared at him.

''Y-yes, I'd like that, Thane,'' Judy said in a

hoarse voice straining with tears. "I'd very much enjoy talking to you about the past...our past."

Paige rose. "If you'll excuse me, I'm going to the refurbished den. I have a lot of things to do to prepare for your first P.T.—physical therapy—session with Jennifer Logan tomorrow morning, Thane." She quickly placed her empty teacup on the tray and gave both of them what she hoped was a look that would invite them to talk intimately with one another.

Before Thane could object to her departure, Paige was gone. He saw Judy's face fall as she looked to the door Paige had exited through. He saw the naked fear in her eyes as she turned and looked back at him. She was gripping the fragile cup between her hands as if trying to steel herself against one of his tirades.

What kind of a bastard was he? Sitting there, he began to realize the enormous damage he'd done by acting out his anger against his mother during the years he'd been forced to live under her roof. And Paige was someone he trusted. If she said he didn't know the truth, then he needed to find out what it was.

"I've been told," he began in low tone, "that I don't know the real story of why you left Dad." Placing the teacup back on the tray beside his bed, he forced himself to hold her gaze. "And since I'm going to be here for a while, I think it's time we talked, don't you? I don't want any anger between us, Mother. What didn't I know that I should know about that divorce?"

Drawing in a deep breath, Judy slowly stood up.

She had arthritis in her right hip and it took some time until she could straighten to her full height. Walking slowly toward Thane, she placed her own cup on the tray. All the while she held his searching green gaze.

"Thank you for giving me the opportunity to tell you," she began in a strained tone. "I never expected it from you…but I'm grateful." She waved her hand nervously in the air.

"I had a certain someone nail me one day about it," he told her ruefully, without mentioning Paige's name. "I trust her with my life and I know she wouldn't lie to me, Mother. She said I didn't know the real reason why you divorced Dad." His mouth compressed. "And I want to know the rest of the story. I think I'm old enough, now, to hear it. Don't you?"

Judy's lower lip trembled as she whispered, "Yes…"

Thane tried to protect himself against anything she might say. His father was like a god to him, just as Paige had accurately realized. Colin Hamilton was larger-than-life to Thane. He always had been. When he'd died suddenly, of a heart attack, Thane's world had shattered. He felt lost without his father's guiding and supportive presence in his life.

"So, what's the truth, Mother? What didn't I know?"

Girding herself, Judy rested her hands lightly against the rail. "It's so painful to tell you, Thane. I know how much you idolized your father. How much he was a hero in your eyes, and your heart. There was a side to him that was heroic. He was a man of great courage. He risked his life many times as a marine. And that part of him you should always hold close to your heart and in your memory. No one is all bad or good—ever.'' She tried to smile, but failed. ''I know there's a part of him I'll always love even now, even after his death at such a young age....''

Thane's gaze dug into her watery eyes. ''Well...if you love him even now, why'd you divorce him? I don't understand.'' The words came out low and strangled.

Judy moaned a little and raised her eyes toward the ceiling. Her hands tightened on the railing. ''Because, Thane, there was a side to your father you never saw...and it was because of that that I left him and took you with me. I had to protect you....''

Giving her a strange look, Thane rasped, ''Protect me? How? From what? Him?''

''Please,'' she begged brokenly, ''hear me out, and then you can judge for yourself, Son. What you didn't know, and what I hate to tell you even now because I know how much you loved and idolized him—'' she took a deep, ragged breath and went on in a low voice ''—was that he had constant love affairs with other women during our marriage.''

Thane's eyes narrowed.

''And when I found out about them—not that he ever tried to hide the fact he was having an affair— he would beat me up. He thought that I'd stop asking questions if he pushed me around, struck or hurt me.''

''What?'' The word came out hoarsely.

Judy held his widening gaze. She saw the shock in Thane's eyes. ''Yes,'' she continued in a steady tone, one that was stronger. "Do you remember when you were a little boy and you saw bruises on my face or arms? Remember you'd ask me about them as I made you breakfast?"

Rapidly, Thane searched his stunned memory. Opening his hands, he looked down at them. "Why...yes, I do remember...."

"And when you asked me about them, I'd always tell you I fell down the stairs or bumped into something?"

Thane ruthlessly culled those memories from his brain. There were many of them. Pain flashed through him. His father an abuser. Having affairs. How could he? How could he have hit his mother like that? Thane couldn't deny his memories. At least two or three times a year, his mother would come out to the kitchen in the morning to make him breakfast, and she'd have a black eye. Or he'd see deep, dark bruises on her arms. And then more memories—worse ones—bubbled up. Jerking his head up, he held his mother's tear-filled eyes.

"What about your two broken arms? I remember when I was ten or so, you broke each of your lower arms." He pointed to them. "Don't tell me..."

Judy nodded, the silence thick with tension. "Your father came home very late that night. He'd been out with his latest affair and came home roaring drunk. We had a fight in the bedroom. I always made sure that you never heard us arguing. I wanted to protect you, Thane. Your father went out of control when I challenged him about having an affair. I told him to get out and never come back. He just laughed at me and started down the hall toward your room. He said if he left, you were leaving with him. I tried to stop him at the bedroom door, and he swung around and shoved me against the wall.'' She held up her left arm. ''That was when I broke it. Well, it shocked him enough to stop him from leaving and trying to take you with him. I went to the hospital the next morning and lied and told them I fell. They set it in a cast and I came home.''

''And the second time?'' Thane recalled she'd suffered a nasty fracture of her right arm when he was twelve years old. As a matter of fact, he recalled that about a week after the break his mother had filed divorce papers on his father.

''Your father was drunk again. He came home and we got into one of our usual fights in the bedroom. I had had it with him having love affairs on the side and flaunting them in my face. I knew you were getting old enough that I wouldn't any longer be able to protect you from this side of your father. I was tired of being abused by him, Thane. And I was so afraid that he'd turn on you, eventually. I was afraid that when you found out he was having affairs, that your love and idolizing him would shatter. I didn't want that to happen. Your father refused to change, and he didn't want to give up his affairs.'' Reaching out, Judy took a huge risk and touched Thane's shoulder. ''I'm so sorry to have to tell you these things. I know how much it hurts you. And I never wanted you to see any side of your father other than his good side, his heroic side. I tried to protect you the best way I knew how. I was desperate. I had to escape him. I knew if I stayed, he'd put me into the hospital, Thane, and I was worried he'd go after you, too, eventually.''

Deeply shaken, Thane felt the explosion of pain and shock roll through him. Paige had been right. He hadn't known the whole truth. The trembling touch of his mother's hand on his shoulder made him feel guilty, too. When he saw the tears drifting down her drawn cheeks, he couldn't stop tears from entering his eyes, too.

''I—I didn't know....'' he began hoarsely.

''I didn't *want* you to know.'' Judy sniffed. She removed her hand and pulled a tissue from her pocket to dab at her eyes and blow her nose.

''In some ways, I wish you had, Mother. It would have helped me understand so much....''

''You were just an innocent child in all of that mess,'' Judy whispered, her eyes red rimmed. ''I'd rather bear your anger than make you lose faith in your father. Like I said before, he *was* a heroic man. A very brave warrior.''

Choking back more tears, Thane hung his head. ''I need to feel my way through this, Mother....''

''I understand, honey. I'll leave you now. If you want to talk more, let me know. Otherwise...I'll leave you in Paige's and Jennifer Logan's capable hands....''

He watched as she picked up the tray. There was such sadness in her face. He felt it in his heart. As she moved toward the closed door, he called out in a strained tone, ''Wait....''

Judy halted and slowly turned around. The look on her son's face was one of anguish. The suffering he was going through made her want to sob. Sometimes the truth hurt—like a knife scoring a person's heart—and she knew that Thane was suffering right now. "Yes?" Her voice was off-key. She needed a good cry—alone, as was her habit.

"You don't have to be a ghost in your own house," he muttered. "Just give me some time to think through all this. And then maybe we can talk more?"

Heartened, she lifted one corner of her mouth. "Yes, I'd like that, Son. Very much…"

Chapter Seven

"Damn…" Thane whispered, gritting his teeth as he finished the last exercise with his injured leg. Sitting on a chair, he allowed the aching extremity to rest gently on the highly polished cedar floor. At his feet, Paige smiled gamely up at him. Sweat rolled off his temples and down his jawline. He relaxed the white-knuckled grip he had on the sides of the chair.

"Great, Thane. You did it!" Paige said, rising to her full height and handing him a small towel. Jennifer Logan had shown him several exercises and it was up to Paige to see that he faithfully did them and to be his coach. She loved being in that role for him.

"Thanks…" He mopped his wrinkled brow with the towel. "I never realized how hard this would be, to bring this leg back to full strength."

Paige went to the window and opened it. The early morning September breeze drifted in. Outside, it was another sunny day with the temperature hovering around fifty, though Paige knew that by noon it would warm up to the eighties. The room was a little too warm and stuffy, already, and Thane was sweating profusely from the mandatory exercises he performed every morning. Turning, she stood by the window watching him. He was dressed in gray sweatpants and a white T-shirt that showed off his magnificent chest and broad shoulders.

"You're making progress," she said. "And I know the exercises hurt your leg, but it will be worth it." Paige tried to sound cheerful and upbeat about it. And she tried to keep their relationship professional, though she had never forgotten his tender, unexpected kiss. How badly she yearned for more, but she was too frightened to trust her heart to him. The sooner Thane's leg got back into shape, the sooner he'd be leaving Sedona—and her—forever. Heart twinging, Paige tried not to look at that too closely right now. He was a month into his recovery at the ranch and doing wonderfully. In fact, he was ahead of schedule, according to Dr. Briggs and Jennifer Logan. His sheer determination—the fact he pushed himself to his absolute limit, physically speaking—was the reason.

Wiping his mouth, Thane glanced over at her. The morning sun was behind Paige, shooting through the panes of the window and backlighting her. It was so hard not to stare like a hungry wolf at her. He had been spoiled with her living at the ranch house, a room away from him. The last month had been heaven for him—and hell.

"Yeah, well, I intend to keep ahead of schedule. I'm not letting Dr. Briggs talk me into staying here for a year in order to get back on my feet." Next week, he went for his second surgery. There was a wheelchair next to him and he reached for it. Releasing the brake on one wheel, he eased it around. Paige came forward to help him shift from the wooden chair where he sat, back onto his "mount," as he referred to the wheelchair.

She held it steady for him as he moved with confidence. Next, he would go to the bench at one end of the room and begin his morning workout routine to keep his upper body in top form.

"Dr. Briggs said that because you were in such great shape when the injury happened, he thinks you'll beat the one-year estimate, too."

Turning the wheels with his gloved hands, he nodded grimly. Pulling up parallel to the leather-covered bench, he growled, "I miss the Corps. I miss everything about it. I'm not about to stay here and waste away."

Paige watched Thane as he placed the brake on the wheel and transferred himself to the bench, straddling it with his thick, hard thighs. He had no idea how powerful or appealing he was to her. None at all. Oh, she'd seen the banked coals of desire burning in his eyes at times when she caught him staring at her. The way he hungrily looked at her in those stolen moments always shook her. Yet ever since that spontaneous kiss at the hospital, he'd never tried to kiss her again. Well, she had no one but herself to blame for that because he'd told her if she wanted him to kiss her, she'd have to initiate it.

Paige pulled the wheelchair away from the bench and handed him a pair of fifteen-pound dumbbells. He took them from her, his fingers touching hers briefly. How she looked forward to this "accidental" contact. What would his fingers be like arching across her skin and worshipping her once more, as if she were the priceless gift she'd felt like when he'd kissed her that one time? Why was she such a dolt? Why did she lie awake for a good hour after going to bed at night, replaying that kiss and what *might* have happened? What it might have led to? A huge part of her wanted Thane to love her outright, regardless of the fact that he would be leaving her at some point, never to return. But the wounded part of her, the part that had been hurt by her marriage, told her that her heart couldn't stand the loss of the only man she had ever truly loved.

Fighting herself on these issues, Paige longed to throw caution to the wind and tell Thane to love her; longed to initiate an intimate relationship with him even knowing he would leave her in the end. But her wounded side cowered at that possibility. Was it better to leave her love of Thane unfulfilled? Untouched? Unstirred? And be content with that one branding, soul-melting kiss he'd shared with her?

Paige pushed the wheelchair aside, focusing once more on Thane's workout. Her duties were to give him the heavier dumbbells after he completed repetitions with the lighter ones. She watched as he lay down on his back like a powerful cougar stretching out in the sun to warm himself. The look in his eyes was one of challenge. His mouth was set. She watched as the biceps in his thickly muscled arms bunched as he began his repetitions. Did he know he was dessert for her eyes and heart? If he had any idea how much she loved to simply watch him, he'd probably be embarrassed. Feeling guilty, Paige looked away. Frowning, she felt torn and unsure of herself. To love and then lose him? Or to love not at all because she was a coward at heart?

Judy entered the room.

"Hi, you two," she greeted them with a warm smile.

Paige lifted her head and said, "Good morning."

"Hi, Mom."

Judy leaned against the doorjamb, her well-worn black Stetson cowboy hat in hand. Her hair was ruffled and her jeans dusty. "Don't kill yourself, Thane."

He blew out a breath of air and kept up the reps. Sweat leaked into his eyes and he blinked it away. "Don't worry, hard work *never* killed me."

Laughing, Judy said, "Coulda fooled me. Hey, I've got a vet emergency." She hooked her thumb across her shoulder. "A cow that's in serious trouble in labor. I'll be out at the barn. Paige, if you see Doc Hazelton, the vet, just send him down there, okay?"

"Sure, no problem." Paige would have liked to offer to help her, which she often did, but she couldn't because Thane needed her help at the moment, too.

"Good," Judy said. "Thanks...gotta run." She threw the hat on her head and moved quickly down the hall.

Thane slowly sat up and handed Paige the dumb-bells. "Thanks," he murmured. Taking the towel, he mopped his face and laid it across his thigh. Glancing at the door where his mother had stood moments before, he said, "I never realized how hard she works."

Paige handed him the next set of dumbbells, which weighed twenty pounds apiece. "I don't know how she does it," she admitted, worry in her tone. "She's fifty-eight, handling a thirty-year-old's level of work and hours."

Thane nodded and lay back down on the bench. "She's got one helluva work ethic, that's for sure." Since their first talk a month ago, the strain between Thane and his mother had dissolved to a great degree. He often asked her to come in, and they'd talk for hours at a time about the past, about his father. It had been hard for Thane at first, because he didn't want to believe that his dad could have done those things. His own memory, however, convinced him that his mother was not lying. He vividly recalled the bruises on her arms and around her neck, and the two broken arms. It sickened him that his father had hurt her like that. In the end, he accepted his mother's story. He had no choice. And his father was no longer the god he'd thought he was.

After the last set of reps, he gave Paige the dumb-bells and sat there, breathing hard. He had to give his muscles time to recuperate. Wiping his face, he smiled up at her. She always stood nearby, her hands clasped in front of her, attentive, yet like a shadow. Today she wore a pale pink angora sweater with a cowl neck that emphasized her gold skin. The way the dark brown slacks fit her lean body, and her black hair lay across her shoulders and framed her face, made him ache to take her in his arms and kiss her. How often he had wanted to crush that sweet, soft mouth of hers against his again.

Thane had to continually remind himself that it was up to Paige to initiate a kiss next time around. Sometimes he saw such longing in her cinnamon-colored eyes, and other days, such sadness. He often wanted to ask what she was feeling at those times. During the month they'd spent together, they'd formed a tentative relationship, but often they were as wary as two fighters circling one another. There was such sweet, sensual energy around her. Did Paige realize that? She reminded him of a flower full of nectar—and he, the starving bee coming to take it from her.

"Why doesn't she hire a man to help her?" he asked Paige as she sat down on the floor nearby.

"She can't afford it, Thane." Paige gave him a frustrated look. "We've had two years of drought and that's stopped grass from growing and made feeding the cattle more difficult. Whatever extra money she had went to feed the livestock, or they'd have died. And if she sold off too many of her cows, she would lose out long term because there wouldn't be enough replacement calves to keep the numbers high enough to be able to pay the bills on the ranch."

"Damned if you do and damned if you don't," he muttered, wrapping the towel around his fists and staring down at it. "And she's raising them without any vaccines or hormone shots, right?"

"Yes. She's been creating a market for organically

raised beef. It's taken years for her to do so, but now, with all the problems with meat, the organic market is finally taking off.''

''And the drought years are really cutting into any profit she might have made from it. I see....'' Thane scowled. There was no doubt his mother needed a man's help around here. In the past month he'd seen how hard she worked to keep her dream alive. This ranch was her heart. Her soul. Thane had never realized any of this until their evening talks revealed these things about her. Because he'd always been his father's pride and joy, Thane had never really bonded with his mother. Now he was doing just that, and it left him concerned for her welfare, because she was working very hard for a woman her age.

Looking at Paige, he studied her serene face and those huge, intelligent brown eyes of hers. ''I know you do a lot to help her out when you're here on the weekends.''

''Yes, I do. And sometimes, if we can swing it, my sisters will come over, too. They're used to ranching, and among the four of us, we can get the heavy or the tricky stuff done.''

''I never realized all this,'' he murmured, looking at the opposite wall, which was painted a pale blue color. The pictures on it were of botanical flowers. All by Victorian artists, of course.

Paige nodded and compressed her lips. ''You know what would be nice?''

''What?'' Thane slanted a glance at her. There was trepidation in her eyes.

''If you decided to stay. I know you love the Marine Corps, but now that you know your mother needs your help, a man's help, you might consider switching careers and coming home permanently.'' Paige knew she was risking everything by putting her own hopes into words. If Thane would stay, then they had a chance at a relationship, too. Possibly. Paige did not fool herself about that, either. It was one thing to dream about being with Thane as a teenager. It was quite another to foster such idealistic expectations as an adult. The real world didn't allow for such fantasies. But if he stayed, at least she'd have a chance to see if he could love her at all. And if he could, then there was a spark of hope for them. Her heart pounded briefly, underscoring the boldness of her comment. She saw his face darken as he carefully considered her words.

His fists tightened around the damp, nubby towel. Wiping his furrowed brow he said, ''I can see she needs help....''

''It would be so wonderful if you could come home,'' Paige whispered. She clasped her hands in unabashed hope.

Wincing, Thane straightened up and moved his shoulders, as if shaking off that possibility. He saw the golden flash in her widening eyes. The way her lips parted. The sudden hope in her gaze. ''Don't say anything to my mother about this, okay? I can't do it. I've got a career in the Corps.'' He wiped his neck. ''I've got early major's leaves coming....'' Seeing the hope snuffed out of Paige's eyes, he felt his heart twinge. He was going to have to leave her, too. The knifelike sensation in his gut made him frown.

''But...'' Paige whispered helplessly, opening her

hands in supplication "...couldn't you be happy here, too, Thane? You're getting along so well with your mother now. You know what really happened all those years ago. She loves you. She always has. And she's spoken to me at times about her wish that you might come home someday and live here with her, make a life in Sedona. She worries who she might pass the ranch on to when she dies. And I know she wishes it would be you...." In her thoughts, Paige selfishly added her own wish that Thane would stay here, too—for her. For their potential love.

Sighing raggedly, Thane growled, "It can't be done."

"Why? Because you want to follow in your father's footsteps and be a career military man?"

Cutting her a sharp glance, he saw the stubborn set of her small chin, her compressed lips. Stung by her question, he said, "It's all I have." And it was. All he'd ever wanted was to be like his father in all ways. A courageous warrior. A marine. And to be seen as brave and bold as his father had been by his own peer group.

Lowering her lashes, Paige whispered, "I understand...." And she did. She saw daily how Thane wrestled with the fact that his father had had feet of clay. She could almost see Thane weighing and measuring himself against the yardstick of his dad's long shadow. And she saw the disappointment in Thane's eyes ever since learning the truth about him. Of course, Thane didn't want to be completely like his father anymore. And sometimes he would speak to her about his conflicting emotions. Paige was always careful not to make blatant remarks about any decision he should come to about his life. In time, he would reach a point where he'd decide to either continue to emulate his father or—what she hoped for—he would learn to separate himself as an individual from the fantasy image he had held all his life, and carve out the life *he* wanted, instead.

Biting on her lower lip, she felt the heat of his gaze still upon her. She wanted to say so much to him about this, yet she knew better. People grew and changed when they internalized the changes themselves. Motivation never came from outside a person. Paige herself had come to understand why she had stayed in her abusive marriage. Eventually she had realized that she didn't have to take such constant pain and hurt from another human being. But she had had to realize it herself. And until she did, her two sisters and their comments made no impression on her at all.

"What about you, Paige? What do you want out of life? Did you have a dream yourself? Have you gotten everything you want?"

His questions were quietly spoken. Searching. She knew he was exploring once again. He had often asked her such questions, and she understood that he only wanted her answers so he could compare them to his own experiences and dreams. Lifting her head, she melted beneath his forest-green gaze. At moments like this, when she saw the thoughtful, sensitive man beneath the warrior's armor he lived within, she loved him so much it hurt.

"Me? Well, my dreams didn't exactly mirror reality," she admitted softly. Paige hesitated a long time, debating whether she should tell Thane anything. She was so ashamed of her past. But the tender flame burning in his eyes, the realization that he did want to know and that he cared, gave Paige the nudge she needed. Opening her hands, she said, "I'm not proud of my past, Thane. In fact…" She rolled her eyes and looked up at the ceiling for a moment. "I made a terrible mistake, and I don't want you to think less of me…."

Thane stopped himself from reaching out to touch her hand. "Listen, we all make mistakes, Paige. No one's perfect."

Rubbing her wrinkled brow, Paige murmured, "Well, then, I guess I've made worse mistakes than most."

"Tell me? I'm here for you, too, you know."

She met and held his warm gaze. Her heart pounded with fear of what he might think of her once he knew the truth. Or how he might judge her, as some of the people around her did. It was that slight movement of his head to one side, his compassionate gaze, that pushed her forward. Gulping unsteadily, she whispered, "I married right out of high school. Johnny Chee proposed to me, and I guess, in a moment of depression mixed with desperation, I said yes."

"Did you love him?" Thane vaguely recalled Chee. He was part Navajo, like Paige, and he'd also gone to their high school. But he was a bully. And he had a nasty mouth. Thane had never liked him because of that.

Shrugging, Paige said, "No…but he said he loved

me. I guess that was enough for me at the time, and I said yes.''

Frowning, Thane said, ''Well, if you didn't love him, why did you marry him?''

''I—well…I loved someone else…and it could never be. I felt as if my whole life were taken away from me, and I was feeling very alone, I guess. Looking back on it, I realize I was a very naive and idealistic eighteen-year-old who didn't know a thing about what really mattered. I was just feeling so torn, so abandoned, that when he came and asked me, I thought that at least one person in the world loved me, and that would be enough.''

Swallowing hard, Thane rasped, ''I see.…'' Who was the man she had loved like that? He relentlessly searched his mind and came up with no one. But noting the pain in her face, he decided not to pry any further, for he had no wish to hurt Paige. She was the single bright light in his life right now and he wanted to see a smile on her oval features and sunlight dancing in her eyes.

''It gets worse,'' Paige warned him wryly. ''I'm afraid getting married was the worst mistake I've ever made. Johnny turned out to be abusive to me. He started beating me up almost daily. I couldn't understand it. I didn't know what I'd done so wrong.'' She saw anger come to Thane's eyes. Holding up her hands, she said, ''I know it was a bad scene, Thane. And if it weren't for your mother, who recognized abuse and saw the bruises on my arms and face, I probably would never have gotten up the courage to leave him.''

''My mother helped you?'' Well, of course, that

made sense now. His father had abused her and she'd be the first to recognize such signs in another woman.

Paige touched her brow nervously. "Actually, she saved my life, Thane. This is something else you should know about your mother. She was so wonderful to me...." Closing her eyes, she pressed her hands against her face and whispered, "This is so awful...no one knows about this except my sisters and your mother...."

Thane grimaced. His stomach automatically knotted. Unable to stand it any longer, he gently pulled her hands from her anguished face. Her eyes were dark with pain. Holding her hands gently in his, he rasped, "Talk to me, Paige. Whatever you say stays with me. You can trust me...."

They were just the words she needed to hear. Paige gripped his hands momentarily, unable to look at him. In an off-key tone, she said, "I didn't cook the eggs right for Johnny one morning. He got really angry at me and pushed me away from where I stood at the stove. I lost my balance and hit the side of the table with my belly. I was three months pregnant and didn't know it. Though I was hurt, I got up and left because it was Saturday morning and I had to be over at your mom's house to do the cleaning. When I drove over here, I began bleeding. Badly. I didn't understand what was going on. I guess I looked pretty pasty to Judy, because when I walked in, she asked me what was wrong. Well, I was so ashamed of myself, she had to drag it out of me.

"In the meantime, I told her I was bleeding. I was confused. I told her I hadn't had a period in three months, and Judy got alarmed. About that time, I had horrendous pain and buckled over. I fainted on the floor. The next thing I knew, I was on a gurney in an ambulance, with Judy and a paramedic sitting beside me. At the hospital, I found out that I'd miscarried my baby.''

"Paige…"

She held his anguished stare. "I know," she whispered unsteadily. "I feel so guilty…so ashamed…. But there's more you need to know. Your mom never left my side. She called the police. She made sure that I didn't have to go back to the house, back to Johnny. She gave me the courage to press charges against him and she supported me all the way. And she gave me a place to stay until the divorce was final." Paige swept her hand around the room. "She let me stay with her. That was what bonded us, Thane. Judy understood, because she'd been there. And she knew what I needed in order to heal and to get a healthy attitude toward any man I might meet in the future." Giving him a slight, one-cornered smile, Paige said softly, "Your mother is a heroine in my eyes, Thane. She walks on water as far as I'm concerned. Without her help, her guidance and wisdom, I wouldn't be where I am today."

Sucking in a deep breath, Thane stared down at her. "I didn't know, Paige. Damn, I'm sorry you lost your baby." And he was. Children were so precious. Someday, he wanted a couple of his own to raise. He'd like to put a fist right through Chee's face right now. Anger warred with his sympathy for Paige. He saw in her eyes that the old wounds were still there. And yet he marveled at how she had bounced back so positively from such an experience. Realizing that his mother had a lot to do with Paige's growth and healthy emotional state, he shook his head. "The more you share with me about my mother, the more I think she's an extraordinary person. I'm just sorry I never appreciated her...as a kid."

"Well," Paige said gently, "you have that opportunity now, Thane. Take advantage of it. Of her. She's got such wisdom. Family is so important. Take it from one who knows. Navajo people have such close-knit families. Everyone lives in the hogan— several generations together." She smiled a little. "And Navajo honor, deeply, their parents' wisdom. The elders couldn't have survived life as long as they have without knowing how to get through it in one piece."

Stunned by all these revelations, Thane sat there digesting her words for a long moment. The sun had moved and the light coming through the window made the reddish-gold cedar floor shine. The autumn sky outside was a bright blue.

Unwrapping the towel from around his fists at last, he settled it across his thigh. Paige smoothly unwound from her position on the floor, ready to assist him as he started his next set of reps. Just the way her black, shining hair cascaded across her proud shoulders filled him with an ache. How badly he wanted to kiss her, to make the pain in her eyes go away.

Reaching out as she straightened, wrapping his fingers gently around her slender wrist, he rasped, "Come here...."

Shaken, Paige froze as his fingers clasped her wrist, his touch firm, yet gentle. Looking down into his eyes, she saw they were wide with sympathy and longing—for her. Mouth dry, she hesitated. He wanted to kiss her. She could see it clearly in his upturned face as his eyes searched hers. Heart bounding, Paige felt all her panic dissolving beneath that hooded, burning look. She needed him so badly. How long she had ached to be in his arms one more time! And after admitting the horror of her past, the loss of her baby, she needed to be closer to him, and allowed herself to settle on the bench in front of him.

Easing his hands upward and framing her face, he saw the sudden shyness, the anxiety and the desire in her half-closed eyes. Several strands of her silken, thick hair slid between his fingers as he drew her face gently toward his.

"I want to kiss you, Paige...."

Her breath caught. Her heart raced. Wild, searing heat moved straight down through her to her belly. A burning sensation, a gnawing need, flowed like lava throughout her body. She sat between his powerful thighs, her hands tightly clasped in her lap. Shivering with need, she nodded her head slightly within his hands. How badly she needed to touch him, to kiss him, to tell him of the love she held only for him—the love he could never know about.

"Good..." he said roughly as he leaned forward, his eyes closing. He brushed her parting lips gently with his own. Remembering how badly she'd been hurt by another man, he placed a tight rein on his boiling, painful need of her. He felt Paige tremble slightly as he grazed her lips. Opening his eyes, he whispered, "Don't be afraid of me, sweet woman. I won't hurt you...I won't cause you pain...." And he wouldn't. That was the *last* thing Thane ever wanted to do.

He felt a soft rush of warm air move against his cheek as he leaned down to recapture her parting, moist lips. Somehow, Thane wanted to absorb all the hurt that she'd experienced. As his mouth met and glided against hers this time, he felt her lean forward and place her hands tentatively on his arms. Her touch was light, hesitant, as if she didn't know whether to flee from him or remain where she was. The softness of her mouth, her shallow breathing, all conspired to make him aware of her in every way.

Paige soaked up his strong, cherishing mouth as it captured hers firmly. She felt the controlled power of Thane, the way he framed her face with his large, scarred hands, the roughness of his skin against her own. Her fingers crept shyly up his arms until she had partially encircled his broad shoulders. Moaning as his tongue moved across her lower lip, Paige surrendered completely to him, in every way. No longer did fear make her hesitant. No, this was what she wanted—this man whom she loved unequivocally. Releasing her face, he wrapped his arms around her and she found herself pressed tightly against his upper body. The feeling was wonderful and protective. Her mind whirled with sensations.

Thane held her as if she were fragile glass that might break at any moment. He cherished her lips, teethed her lower lip gently and then rocked her mouth open even more. The moment his tongue slid against hers, she moaned. It was a moan of utter pleasure, not rejection. He lifted his mouth from hers. They were breathing hard and raggedly. Lifting her lashes, she met his slitted green gaze and burned beneath it. Feeling his hands move across her back and hips, she raised her chin and closed her eyes. How badly she wanted to love him completely, to go all the way with him. The ache in her lower body intensified until all she could feel was a sense of longing for him more powerful than anything she had felt in all her life.

As if he was reading her thoughts, his hand glided smoothly around her rib cage and caressed the side of her firm, aching breast beneath the soft angora sweater. Uttering a sigh, Paige sank her own fingers into his tightly bunched shoulders. Just the simple touch of his hand on the side of her breast made her go weak with need.

Thane had to control himself. He had to stop. Lifting his hand from where he cupped her full breast, he gave her an unsteady smile, one corner of his mouth lifting. "You're too much of a temptation," he told her in a low tone. Keeping his hands on her upper arms, he eased her away from him. Paige's face was flushed. Her lips were wet and parted. Her eyes were soft and dappled with gold, telling him she'd enjoyed the kiss as much as he had. "If I don't stop now, sweetheart, I won't stop at all...."

Understanding all too well, Paige placed her hand against her brow and tried to reorient herself to reality. Her body was exploding with tiny tremors and aches of neediness for him alone. She couldn't share any of that with him because she knew he would eventually leave her and go back to the Marine Corps. "I—I know," she said, her voice off-key and trembling. So much needed to be said. Yet as Paige dropped her hand away from her brow and drowned in his burning green gaze, she felt helpless to deny Thane anything. Swallowing erratically, she moved away from him. She regretted the loss of his large hands on her arms, but it couldn't be helped. Was she strong enough emotionally to love him while he was here and release him when he wanted to leave?

Chapter Eight

Why was Paige so distant with him? Thane wondered as he hobbled on crutches into the living room, where he and his mother were sharing a glass of deep red Syrah wine to celebrate New Year's Eve. The pleasant snap and crackle of the fire that greeted him was soothing as he entered the room. Two of the hand-painted Victorian puffy lamps cast low shadows, and soft classical music wafted through the warm room. When he saw his mother sitting by herself in a wing chair, the slender stem of a wineglass between her fingers, he gave her a worried look.

"I thought Paige was joining us?"

"I did, too. I told her she didn't have to do the dishes right now."

"I'll go get her," Thane said, and swung toward the door that led to the kitchen. Every time he put weight on his right foot, pain arced up through his calf. He'd gotten used to it over the past months. Dr. Briggs had said he'd have a helluva lot of pain; well, the doctor had been right, as usual. Still, Thane's leg was coming back and that was the best news.

Pushing the swinging door aside with his elbow, he managed to make it into the narrow kitchen. Paige was at the sink, a bright pink apron wrapped around her waist. He halted. How beautiful she looked to him. She'd worn her hair up and decorated it with the bright, colorful silk scarf he'd gifted her with at Christmas. Her dark red, velvet dress had a scoop neck, and long sleeves that she'd pushed up to her elbows in order to do the dishes. The dress hung gracefully across her wide hips, falling to her slender ankles, and the rich color enhanced her golden flesh, filling him with a desire to touch her.

"Have I told you how beautiful you look tonight?"

Paige turned and gave him a brief smile of welcome. She blew a strand of dark hair away from her damp brow. "No, but it's nice to hear it. Thank you." How handsome Thane looked in the cream-colored cable knit sweater and dark brown slacks. She thrilled to the way he looked at her as he stood there at the door on his crutches. She knew that look well by now, saw it every day as she worked with him in rehab: he wanted to kiss her. But ever since the second kiss they'd shared, Paige had become frightened. He never made a move to try and kiss her again. Paige was relieved in one sense, because it meant she was in control of whatever their relationship was to become.

Moving over to the table, Thane sat down. "Want some help drying?"

"Ohh...no. I'll just put the dishes in the drainer and they can air dry. Thanks..." Paige was struck by Thane's willingness to help her with such activities. Maybe he was bored. For sure, he was restless. He was unable to go outside in the cold with his crutches, and she knew he felt cooped up. One slip on the ice or snow and he could permanently damage his healing leg. The second surgery had only been four weeks ago. And more than anything, Thane wanted that leg to heal so he could leave for the Marine Corps.

"That was a great meal you two put together," he said, hungrily absorbing her form as she worked at the sink. There was never any wasted movement where Paige was concerned. He enjoyed every one of her graceful gestures. The Navajo knew how to walk, how to move naturally. They had a grace to them that he'd always admired. Maybe it was their deep connection to the land and all things around them.

"Judy and I had a lot of fun planning it around your favorite foods." She twisted to look over her shoulder. Thane seemed pensive. A little sad, perhaps. He was probably thinking about getting back to his old job at Camp Reed. Of late, he'd been on the phone to his commander at the marine base, which was situated north of San Diego. And he'd been talking to some of the officers of other Recon teams he knew there and had worked with before his injury. She saw how badly he needed that lifeline to them, and it scared and saddened her. As soon as

Thane could get off those crutches and begin walking without them—a day that was coming shortly—she knew he would brutally push himself to get back into peak form. Once that happened, he would be gone— forever—out of her life.

She concentrated on scrubbing the skillet, though her heart squeezed with terror at the thought of his leaving. Should she give herself completely to Thane? What made her think that he'd want her the way she wanted him? Her past had jaded her. On many days, she felt unworthy of him. He was a hero. A genuine hero. She was nothing in comparison. Oh, it was her silly daydreams that made her yearn for him, want to love him and be loved by him. Some aspects of her foolish schoolgirl dreams had never left her. Or, Paige wryly thought, she had just never grown up. She was still trapped by her old love for Thane.

"Tomorrow," Thane told her, "I'm throwing these crutches away." He grinned a little as she looked at him with surprise. "My New Year's wish to myself was that I'd walk by January 2 or else."

Swallowing in surprise, Paige said, "Isn't it a little too soon? Dr. Briggs thought by February—"

Shrugging, Thane restlessly moved the salt and pepper shakers that sat on the table, which was covered with a pink crocheted cloth. "I've always been ahead of Brigg's curve, his expectations for me," he muttered. "I intend to stay that way."

Her heart squeezed in anguish. "That's true," she managed to admit in a strangled tone. Returning to her duties, Paige scrubbed the dishes with renewed nervous energy. Thane would leave sooner, not later.

Closing her eyes, she took in a deep, ragged breath. She was such a coward! Why couldn't she just throw herself on Thane's mercy and see if he would accept a relationship with her? She was unworthy, she knew, but something was driving her to do just that.

Thane frowned. He saw the terror in Paige's eyes. Why? And he heard her voice go husky with tears. Tears? Again, why? He scowled and moved the sugar bowl aimlessly around on the tablecloth. He wanted Paige so badly he could taste her. How many nights had he lain awake, knowing she was only a room away from him? And how many times had he entertained the thought of going to her room and asking her to share his bed? Maybe because of her abusive past, she was scared of him? After all, he was a man. A big, tall man, at that. Maybe his height scared her. Did Paige think he'd hurt her as Johnny had? Was she able to separate him from her ex-husband? So many questions and no answers. And he was afraid to ask, for fear of what her answer would be. He was the ultimate coward, he decided unhappily. He could face a wall of bullets, but not her possible answer.

"When you're done, would you like to share some wine with us?" Thane asked her hopefully.

"No...thank you. I don't drink alcohol. My Indian blood stops me from doing it."

"That's right...I forgot. Sorry." *Damn*. He was putting his foot into his mouth every opportunity he got. North American Indians lacked the ability to metabolize alcohol. He should have remembered that. Harshly, Thane told himself he was too insensitive to Paige and that needed to change. He'd been so focused on himself, on his driving need to get well, that he'd pretty much ignored other people's needs.

Paige saw the little-boy look on his face. She thrilled to the fact that when they were alone, Thane removed that tough marine mask and was his easygoing self. Her mouth curved slightly. "I make a mean cup of hot chocolate with marshmallows, though. Interested?"

He gave her a reckless grin. "You bet. Is there anything I can do to help you?"

"No...just sit there and keep me company. Does Judy want to join us?"

Insensitive again. Thane got up. "I'll go ask her."

Paige was placing the last of the dishes in the drainer when Thane hobbled back into the kitchen.

"Mom told me that one glass of wine is putting her to sleep. She said to tell you happy New Year and she'll see us in the morning."

Glancing up at the clock, Paige saw it was 12:30 a.m. "She's way past her bedtime," she murmured.

"I'm still game for that hot chocolate," he reminded her, coming over to the counter near where she stood. He watched as she dried her hands with a white towel that had red candy canes embroidered into it. His mother loved Christmas. And the tree was still up in the living room, a sparkling reminder of the holiday they'd shared together. It had been a good one. Thane had always celebrated Christmas with his father, if possible, though many times, it hadn't been. His father had either been on a mission or at an overseas command. This had been one of the best Christmas holidays Thane could ever recall.

And gazing down into Paige's soft, shy features, he knew in part why.

"Okay, have a seat," Paige murmured, leaning down to pull a pan from beneath the cabinet. "It's too bad Judy can't join us."

Thane nodded. "She looked a little tired from drinking that glass of wine." But then, Judy had dealt with the demands of the ranch all day, too, Thane reminded himself. And she wasn't in her twenties like he was. She did a phenomenal amount of work, and his admiration for her had increased markedly.

Paige smiled softly. "She works so hard...." She turned to busy herself with preparing the chocolate.

Obediently, Thane sat down so he could watch her work, hungrily absorbing her inborn grace. The clinking of the pan and other kitchen sounds relaxed him. He noticed that when Paige was around, he wasn't restless. Only when he was left alone did he feel antsy and unfulfilled.

She placed a spoon and a bright red napkin in front of him, and at the place where she would sit. Catching her sparkling cinnamon-colored gaze, he said, "Have you ever thought of moving away from here?"

Startled, Paige stopped midway to the stove, where the milk was heating in the pan. "Move? Away from *here?* My *home?*" She laughed and raised her hand. "Oh, no. I'd never leave my family, Thane. You know us Navajo—we're bred from Mother Earth and we stay close to her, and close to our family." Shaking her head and chuckling, she moved to the stove and briskly stirred in the chocolate, sugar and salt. She sprinkled a pinch of cinnamon into her recipe.

"You don't have any curiosity about other places? Cities? Countries?"

Shrugging, Paige glanced over at him and said, "Not really. Everything I love is here. Why should I leave? My sisters and I are so close. And the rest of our family—our aunts, uncles and cousins—are on the Navajo Reservation, not far away. They come for regular visits, and we go up to the res to celebrate ceremonies with them."

"Hmm, having family around is a big help," Thane admitted as he played with the spoon she'd given him.

"I know you Anglos hop, skip and jump around the U.S.A. like it's a game," Paige said, "and you don't value family proximity like we do. But I could never leave here...or abandon my family like that."

"Yeah, we've become a restless race, haven't we?" he mused. He liked the way her black hair shone with red highlights beneath the Victorian lamp that hung in the middle of the kitchen.

Taking the pan off the stove, Paige poured the steaming contents into two cream-colored mugs. Setting the pan in the sink, she opened up a package of pink, blue and green marshmallows and added some to both mugs. Bringing the cups over, she set them down. Then, removing the pink apron, she hung it over another straight-backed, cherry wood chair. She grinned and sat down.

"Drink up. I think you'll like it. A great substitute for alcohol."

Picking the mug up, he toasted her. "To the most beautiful woman in the world."

Heat prickled Paige's cheeks. She curved her fingers around the handle of her cup. "I can't be! But thank you, anyway. It's nice to be seen that way." She lifted her cup and took a sip of the rich, warm chocolate, her heart expanding with joy.

Chuckling, Thane saw that the melting marshmallows had created a slender mustache along her upper lip as she set the cup down.

"Come here, sweet woman." He reached out and cupped her face, then moved his thumb gently across her upper lip to remove the evidence. The startled look in her eyes, the heat that built in them, made him throb with the desire to kiss her. After he removed the mustache, he reluctantly removed his hands. Over and over, Thane had to remind himself not to try to control Paige. After she'd told him of the abuse, he'd had more than a few talks with his mother about it—and about Paige. Judy had counseled him to always let her initiate any intimacy; that way, she was not disempowered by him simply charging in like a bull and doing it instead. In order for her to heal, Judy had told him, Paige had to feel confident enough to ask for what she needed from him. Otherwise, there was nothing healthy or positive to build upon.

Tiny prickles of pleasure moved across Paige's upper lip. Feeling bereft as Thane removed his large, strong hands from her face, she looked down to avoid the dark, predatory look in his half-closed eyes. He wanted to kiss her. She wanted to kiss him. She was such a coward. Touching her tingling lip tentatively, she whispered, "Th-thanks...."

The tension built between them. Thane couldn't understand her reaction. Had he insulted her? Shocked her? What had he done wrong? Clearing his throat, he quickly took a gulp of his chocolate. Casting around for a safe topic, he said, "What's your New Year's wish?"

Startled, Paige quickly put her hands around the warm mug. Her heart was pounding with need of Thane. Her lips tingled hotly in the wake of his grazing touch. He was always so gentle with her. She knew in her heart he would never hurt her. At least, not on purpose. "Oh, a silly thing—something that would never come true," she blurted. Why had she said that? Cringing inwardly, Paige died inside. Every time Thane touched her, she melted like the marshmallows in the cup she was gripping for dear life.

"What?" he prodded, watching her closely. The high flush of pink stained her cheeks. She refused to look at him. He knew Paige well enough by now to know that he'd somehow hit on a very tender topic with her. In the past, she would hang her head, avert her eyes and refuse to meet his gaze. In some ways, she was so Navajo, and it was at those times that he felt such a fierce need for her sweep through him.

"N-nothing, really...just a silly schoolgirl's dream, is all. You really wouldn't be interested, Thane." Gulping, she forced herself to look at him briefly. "What about *your* wish? I'll bet it is to be able to leave us and go back to the Marine Corps in three months or less?" Paige tried valiantly to keep the anguish out of her tone and to sound cheerful instead.

She didn't succeed. At all.

Thane tipped his head, hearing the pain in her voice. When he saw tears shimmer in her wide brown eyes, his heart contracted. "Hey, what's this?" Without thinking, he reached over and touched the corner of her eye with his fingers. The tear dripped across them, warm and wet.

Getting up, Paige nearly tipped over the chair. She caught it just in time. "Oh!" Gripping the back, she quickly set it upright. Her face felt like it was on fire. Feeling like a klutz, she was reminded of the times that Johnny would come after her, cornering her so she couldn't run, couldn't escape. Breathing hard, Paige backed up until she bumped into the counter with her hips.

"Easy…" Thane rasped. He was on his feet instantly, without his crutches. Paige looked confused and anxious. What had he said to alarm her? Not understanding, but driven to help her, he stepped toward her, his hand extended. The moment he placed his full weight on his right foot, pain ripped up through it and into his gut. A groan escaped him. He staggered. Blackness swam in front of his eyes. He heard Paige cry out. Falling. He was falling!

Paige grabbed Thane by his arm, breaking his fall to the tile floor. As he fell, he twisted around to land on his left side. His good side. But he was so heavy and tall that his descent jerked Paige off her feet. She landed heavily next to him, her fist still gripping his sweater.

With a gasp, she scrambled to her knees. Thane

was groaning, reaching out toward his injured leg, his fingers clawlike. Agony masked his features.

"Lie still!" she gasped as she quickly moved to his right leg. He wore a soft, open sandal over a thick, protective sock and an elastic bandage.

All Thane could do was lie there, his head spinning, his senses numbed out by the unexpected pain. He felt Paige leaning over him, her touch gentle as she pulled his pant leg upward to examine his right leg. Breathing hard, he kept gasping to stop from crying out. The pain was slowly abating.

"Dammit," he rasped, closing his eyes and trying to fight the blackness rimming his vision.

"It was my fault," Paige rattled. "I'm sorry, Thane—so sorry...." She examined his red, welted calf. It looked okay. Next, she released the pins to the elastic bandage and unwound it expertly. There was no sign of swelling. "Everything looks all right," she told him, giving him a quick glance. Putting the elastic bandage back in place, she whispered, "We need to put ice on it, just in case. Do you feel like standing? I need to get you to your bed so we can work with it. Come on, lean on me. I'll help you up...." And she stood, extending her hand to him.

Thane reached out, his fingers engaging hers. He knew she was a lot stronger than she looked. Putting all his weight on his left leg, he awkwardly rose. With his arm sliding around her shoulders, he steadied himself. Paige was so warm and strong. How often had he wanted to feel her this close to him?

"Here, use this crutch under your left arm," she told him breathlessly as she handed it to him. "Between me and it, we'll get you to your bedroom. If we get ice on that ankle soon enough, we'll stop any swelling before it starts.'' Her heart was pounding nonstop now as she guided him slowly but surely from the kitchen to his bedroom. The light was already on and she gently maneuvered him so he could sit on his bed. His eyes were dark with pain. Feeling badly, she helped Thane lie down. Placing a pillow beneath the heel of his right leg, she rushed out of the room and back to the kitchen to put some ice in a plastic bag.

Lying there, the pain slowly going away, Thane watched as Paige hurried back into his room. Her hair was disheveled, the dark strands loosened by her fall. Worry was clearly etched across her features.

''Are you all right?'' he demanded huskily, reaching out for her.

Paige nodded and gripped his fingers momentarily. ''I'm fine...fine. Let me get ice on your ankle, Thane....''

The tension swirled around them. Thane could have cut it with a knife. His emotions seesawed between worry over any possible damage he'd done to his foot and Paige's overreaction in the kitchen. Something wasn't right, and he felt frustrated not knowing what it was.

''Are you sure you're okay?'' he demanded more strongly as he saw her bandage the ice bag across his ankle.

Lifting her head, Paige stared at him. In the shadowy darkness, relieved only by a small lamp on the bedstand, his face was carved and strong looking. His green eyes were like ebony and glittering with concern—for her. Managing a wobbly smile, she whispered unsteadily, "I'm really okay…it's you I'm worried about. I'm sorry, Thane…so sorry. This is my fault…."

As she completed her task, Thane wasn't about to let her go. "No you don't," he growled, and gripped her by her hand, bringing her around so that she was forced to sit on the edge of his bed and face him. Refusing to release her hand, Thane watched her closely for a reaction. "The last thing I want is for you to be afraid of me, Paige."

She opened her lips to protest.

"No…hear me out, will you?" he said in a low, urgent tone. He felt her fingers relax within his. It was enough to assure him that she didn't want to flee from his side. He felt the clammy dampness of her hand, though, and it made him feel desperate.

"There are times when I touch you, or hold my hand out to you, that you draw back…like—like I'm Johnny. And I'm not, Paige. I'm me. Thane. I would *never* hurt you. Don't you realize that? I'd give anything in this world to see you happy and secure. You deserve nothing but love. One helluva lot of it, as far as I'm concerned. I know you were hurt by him. Badly. And every time I think about it and I see you react to me, it makes me angry. I wish he was around. I'd beat the hell out of him for what he did to you…." Thane wiped his mouth with the back of his hand. Paige had a stunned look on her face. It was now or never, he decided.

"I like you…a lot. And it's driving me crazy to keep my hands off you. Every time I think I've made some progress with you, something I say or do scares you, and you back off from me. I'm feeling frustrated. I *want* to understand, Paige, but it's a two-way street. I'm not about to force myself on you like Johnny did. I want—wish—you'd come to me of your own free will. You don't know how many times I've lain awake in this bed wishing I'd see you at my door, waiting to share yourself with me...."

Paige closed her eyes. She uttered a moan and placed her other hand across her face. Instantly, she felt Thane's hand hold hers more firmly. She clutched at his strong fingers. Her heart pounding in her ears, she felt suddenly weak with shock from his admission. "I—I didn't know, Thane. I never knew you felt like this...." She stopped and forced the words out one at a time. "Toward me..."

Groaning, Thane whispered, "Maybe I've been the damn fool, sweetheart. Maybe I should have told you this sooner, but I was afraid to. I was afraid you'd say no...turn me down, for a lot of reasons...."

Her hand fell away from her face. Paige turned and looked down into Thane's suffering features. "Even now, you're more courageous than I could ever be. I know what kind of bravery it takes to be this honest with another person." One corner of her mouth lifted and she choked out, "I'm afraid, too, Thane. Of so much—but not of you. No, I could never be afraid of you. I never was. How could I be now?" She saw his eyes widen at her admission. His strong lips parted. Releasing her hand, he slowly pulled himself up into a partial sitting position. His gaze was predatory. He was the hunter, she his quarry. But it felt wonderful, not threatening, to Paige.

"I don't deserve a man like you," she continued in a breathless, hushed voice. If she didn't let the words tumble out in a rush, she knew she'd become cowardly once again, and never tell him the truth of how she really felt toward him. "I never did...but I could dream—and did dream—of you...."

"That's not true," Thane muttered, and he gripped her upper arms and gave her a small shake. "Do you think your past stops me from feeling what I do for you? I don't give a damn about you being married before. That doesn't stain you or make you less in my eyes." His fingers stroked her firm flesh. "Paige...look at me, please, sweetheart...look into my eyes, my heart. Is there anything in there that scares you about me?" Relentlessly, Thane held her wide, tear-filled gaze.

Paige felt her heart breaking with anguish. With fear. With joy. Thane's voice shook with emotion. When she saw tears coming to his narrowed eyes, it broke open the last of the fear that had dammed up her heart. Whispering his name, Paige reached out, her fingers grazing his recently shaved cheek. The moment her fingers glided against his skin, his eyes shut tightly. She saw the tears bead along his thick, spiky lashes. Pain flowed through her. She realized how much she had hurt him with her reticence, with her fear of loving him fully.

As she glided her fingers up the hard, clenched line of his jaw, up past his cheek where the scar lay, tangling them into his closely cropped dark hair, she whispered his name once more.

"Do you know that you're a dream come true for me, Thane? Do you know how long I've wanted you, dreamed of you, ached for you? I was scared. So very scared. I didn't think I was worthy of someone like you. The hero. The man who braved death as regularly as I breathed air to live.''

His eyes opened. Thane ruthlessly studied her softened features, her pleading eyes, which sparkled with tears. Just the touch of her trembling fingers grazing his hair, the side of his face, sent a powerful ache surging into his lower body. As her tears drifted down her flushed cheeks, he groaned and released her arms. With his large, thick fingers, he tried to carefully wipe her cheeks.

''Do you know what my New Year's wish was?'' Thane asked her thickly as he framed her face. ''Do you?''

''No....''

''That you would let me love you. Let me show you that a man could be gentle...could treat you like you deserved, and not hurt you. Show you the beauty of a man loving his woman like it should be....''

Her breath hitched. A sob caught in her constricted throat. She'd never seen a man cry before, but Thane was crying—for her. For her past pain. Her fear shattered around her as she held his unsure gaze. She felt his fingers tightening warmly against her face. An arcing joy flowed through her. Stunned by his broken admissions, she eased out of his grip and stood.

Thane swallowed hard and watched as Paige went to the opened bedroom door and quietly shut it, closing them off from the world. The shadows wrapped around her lovingly, the dark red velvet material of the dress outlining her lithe figure. As she turned toward him, her face was a combination of light and darkness. She reached up in a graceful gesture and unpinned her hair. The black strands fell in an ebony waterfall about her shoulders and flowed down across her breasts.

Thane saw the glimmer in her eyes, that never left his as she walked toward him, the silver-and-turquoise hair comb in her fingers. She leaned over and switched off the small lamp on the bedstand. Moonlight, clear and strong, spilled in through the window, making rippling patterns across the floor and his bed through the crocheted Victorian curtains.

As she slowly approached him, he saw the fear, the desire and the love burning in her half-closed eyes. Holding out his hand, he murmured, "Come here...."

Chapter Nine

"I'm afraid, Thane...." Paige managed to get the words out as she sat down facing him, her hand coming to rest on his. His face was in shadows, but she saw the glitter in his eyes, and simultaneously felt an overwhelming sense of protection emanating from him. It gave her the courage to go on. "It's been a long time." She didn't meet his gaze for a moment. "Since Johnny...well, I've avoided men like the plague...."

"Paige..." His words were whispered as he sat up and slid his hand across her cheek. "Look at me, sweetheart...."

She lifted her head and drowned in his darkened eyes. Swallowing convulsively, Paige realized she had never felt the nurturing and warmth that now surrounded her. Only with Thane. When he em-

LINDSAY McKENNA 169

braced her, she felt loved and needed in a way she never had before.

Thane managed a broken smile. "Listen to me, will you?" He stroked her cheek gently. "I'm scared, too, if it makes you feel any better."

Her eyes widened.

Nodding, Thane managed a crooked smile. "When I woke up in that hospital and saw you, my heart went crazy inside my chest. I was so glad to see you again. At that moment, I clung to you like I was a dying man and you were my life raft, my only safety in a world gone mad." He threaded his long, scarred fingers through the loose, silky strands of her ebony hair. "And you've been that for me from that moment up to now. It was a good thing you couldn't read my mind that day, Paige, or you'd have left and never come back."

She heard the self-deprecation in his low tone and it relaxed her. The magic of him simply moving his fingers lingeringly across her scalp eased her panic.

Automatically, Paige leaned against his opened palm as it settled once more against her cheek. "I could never run from you, Thane." Not ever. She loved him. She knew it now as never before. But Paige didn't fool herself this time. She did not mistake Thane's interest in her as love. He'd never said those words to her and she was very sure he wouldn't, because he was going to walk out of her life as soon as his leg was healed. That knowledge hurt her, like a knife shredding her wildly beating heart. But it didn't matter anymore. Paige realized that loving Thane now while he was here with her was the right thing to do. She would have to love and release him. At least she would have a few months with him, a few months of glorious, unfettered love that she could hold in her heart for the rest of her life.

"Well," Thane whispered as he smiled down at her, "you've got more courage than I do." His gaze locked on to her widening brown eyes, which had gold flecks of desire within them. "I want to love you, sweetheart. Right now…" He felt the knot of burning heat building painfully in his lower body. His heart throbbing with a surprising ache he'd never felt before, Thane saw Paige give him a wobbly smile of consent. She was so shy and fragile in those seconds that spun out of time. The moonlight caressed her high cheekbones and made her eyes sparkle. An avalanche of need for her, a fierce desire to protect her, surged through Thane.

"Your leg…" Paige murmured in a strangled tone. "We have to be careful, Thane…."

Grimacing, he nodded. "I know. What I'd like to do is drag you down beside me and love the hell out of you, but I think we'd better be a little more conscious of what we're doing and how we do it."

She laughed slightly and placed her hand against his chest in a gesture that claimed him as her man. It was a bold move on her part, something that she had long wanted to do. "We can't get completely lost in the heat of passion."

Their laughter was soft and broke the tension in the room.

"There's something very provocative about undressing a woman, garment by garment," Thane told her darkly as he eased his hands around her slender neck to locate the zipper of her crushed velvet dress. "You don't know how many times I've dreamed of doing just this to you...."

His fingers found the hidden zipper between her shoulder blades. Paige moved forward so he didn't have to strain to reach it, pressing her brow against his shoulder. Sliding her hand across his well-sprung chest, she felt his breath catch. His reaction was wonderful. Paige hadn't expected it. But then, her dizzied mind told her, this was Thane. Not her ex-husband. She felt the zipper being eased down her spine, her flesh tingling wildly in the wake of the slow, delicious descent.

Thane closed his eyes and pressed his jaw against her head, breathing in the scent of her soft, thick hair. "You smell wonderful. Do you know how many times in that damned hospital I could smell the fresh scent of sage around you? I used to inhale it like an oxygen-starved animal." He smiled and then pressed several small kisses into the soft strands.

Paige felt the dress parting against her back. When he removed his hands, she felt a little nervous. What if she looked ugly to him? Repulsive? Johnny always said her breasts were too small and that she was too wide in the hips. What if she wasn't what Thane expected? Panic surged through Paige. As she gathered the courage to ease upward, she felt Thane bring his hands to her shoulders and ease the crushed velvet downward.

Paige's breath hitched. She wore no bra, only a silken red chemise beneath her dress. As the material was eased away, she felt her breasts firming up and her nipples hardening. Unable to watch Thane's initial reaction to her, she closed her eyes and waited. Her breath caught. What if she was ugly to him?

As the dress pooled around Paige's hips, Thane stared at her lovely form. The red silk chemise only emphasized her proud, small breasts, the nipples pressed urgently against the soft material, telling him that she was waiting for his touch. And he wouldn't disappoint her. Reaching out, he settled his hands on her shoulders. Her skin was warm and firm beneath them.

"You are so beautiful...." he rasped as he eased his hands down to cup and caress her.

A wild, hot feeling zigzagged through her. Paige's lips opened. An explosive breath escaped her. When his thumbs moved across the tight, hard peaks, a weakness assailed her. She moaned softly and pressed herself more urgently into his exploring hands. Thane thought she was beautiful! Relief flooded through Paige, made her joyous. It freed her and made her feel more bold. She opened her eyes and saw the awe, the warmth smoldering in Thane's eyes as she met and held his gaze. Without thinking, for everything she did with him was now becoming instinctual, Paige lifted her hands and gripped the bottom of his sweater.

"Let me touch you," she whispered, and helped him out of the garment. As she lay it to one side, she saw to her pleasure that Thane wore nothing beneath it. The sight of the massive span of his darkly haired chest was thrilling to her heightened senses. Paige boldly placed her hands there. It was one thing to massage him daily as a professional masseuse and nurse. It was quite another to release all her tightly held desires and begin her slow, delicious exploration of him as a male animal she hungered for and wanted to excite.

Groaning, Thane gripped her upper arms momentarily as her fingertips moved with tantalizing lightness across his chest, leaving a trail of fire. He had always enjoyed her professional side as a masseuse, but this was different. Very different. Hungrily, he absorbed her bold exploration of him. He liked Paige's courage, for he'd seen the fear in her eyes earlier. Somehow, his words had erased her fears, and now she was actively engaged in their loving one another. Happiness flowed through him, and Thane smiled as her hands moved downward, toward the waistband of his trousers.

"Lie back," Paige whispered wickedly.

With a sigh, Thane did as she asked. Paige had a glint in her eyes he'd never seen before, and he liked it a lot. The hunted was the hunter now. Her fingertips moved provocatively down across his hard, flat abdomen and tangled with a maddening slowness into the waistband of his trousers. A breath escaped him, more of a groan, as she eased the material apart and began to move it down across his hips and thighs. At one point, Paige stood up. Thane opened his eyes and watched her gracefully remove the red velvet dress from her lean body and lay it across the back of a chair. As she stood before him, dressed in only the crimson silken chemise and bikini briefs, he absorbed the sight of her slender form like a starving wolf.

Moving to the bed, Paige removed his trousers completely, being very careful with his right leg and foot. There was no mistaking the bulge beneath his light blue boxer shorts. As she slid her fingers under the elastic, she watched his expression. His eyes narrowed to slits and burned with fire. For her. Feeling hot and shaky, Paige eased the material downward. Her throat grew constricted as she saw the evidence of his desire for her. It took everything she had within her to finish easing the shorts off his leg.

Paige slowly finished undressing in turn. Thane thought she was beautiful, and that gave her the courage to stand naked before his burning gaze as her lingerie drifted to the floor. She moved to the opposite side of the bed. With his right leg injured, there would be only one way to lay with him—on his left side.

Thane swallowed hard. Moonlight caressed Paige's tall, straight body as she moved silently around the end of the bed. Her black hair cascaded like an ebony river across her shoulders and around her proud breasts. Reaching out, he captured her hand because he saw the unsureness in her eyes.

"I've never seen anyone as beautiful as you are," he said in a rasping tone, and he tugged on her hand.

Encouraged by his words and by the invitation in his fiery green eyes, she slid lithely across the bed. As her long body paralleled his, she felt heat and power emanating from him. How easy it was to allow Thane to slide his arm beneath her neck and shoulder and draw her toward him, then drag her hotly against his awaiting body. Eyes closing, Paige sighed as she felt his masculine power. The moment his mouth grazed her lips, she moaned. Her hand lifted and she moved it down his hard, tense body, from his rib cage to his narrow hip.

Hungrily, she drank of his mouth as it fitted hotly and eagerly against hers. When she eased her hand downward and caressed his hardness, he tensed violently. His mouth crushed hers. His breathing grew ragged. Deep within her, Paige thrilled to his response. Johnny had said she was inept as a lover, that she could never please him. Now Paige realized differently. The man who held her tightly in his arms, who was sharing his breath, his life with her, was responding wildly, beautifully to her small, tentative attempts to please him.

Thane groaned and gripped Paige to him as her fingers caressed and cajoled him. His mind exploded. He tried to get control over himself. She was a surprising and bold lover and he'd been caught completely off guard. Smiling to himself, he eased Paige onto her back. Her black hair spilled like ebony ink across the pillows beneath her. As she slowly opened her eyes, he saw them glitter hungrily. Perspiration dotted his forehead as she continued to touch and tease him.

"You're not getting away with that," he growled, and leaned down and caught her hardened nipple, which was begging to be lavished, in his mouth.

Paige cried out as pleasure rippled from her breasts down to her burning lower body. Instantly, she gripped him, her fingers digging hard into his taut back as he gently assaulted her. Oh! The pleasure! Artlessly, she arched beneath him, his male hardness pressing insistently between her thighs. Moaning again, her head moving from side to side, she didn't think she could stand the radiating heat and sensations as he suckled her other nipple. How badly she wanted Thane! Her mind was shattered; only her primal animal instincts survived his deliberate and slow onslaught.

Moving his strong fingers lightly across her lean rib cage and waist, across her wide hips, he headed with purpose to the V of her thighs. He felt her turn soft and languid within his grip. *Good.* He wanted to please Paige as much as she had pleased him with her boldness. Now it was her turn. Holding her tightly with one arm, her brow pressed against him, he moved his other hand downward and eased her long, curved thighs apart. The moment he met the sweet, wet honey of her body, Thane felt her spine begin to bow into a graceful arch. Her breasts pressed hard against his chest and her fingers dug convulsively into his back.

"Good," he rasped near her ear as he gently continued to explore her, "feel it, Paige…feel the pleasure…."

A scorching wildness licked up through her. As she arched, she cried out and gripped Thane with all her womanly strength, her arms wrapping around his broad shoulders. Golden explosions occurred wherever his fingers grazed her. Her breath was sporadic. The sensations throbbing through her caught her completely off guard. She had no idea what had happened, only that she was spinning out of control, her body hot and explosive in the wake of his teasing.

Laughing huskily, Thane eased back just enough to see her flushed face, her eyes opening with awe and surprise. For a second he wondered why. And then he put it together in his shorting-out mind: Paige had never been pleasured by a man in this way. She had never experienced a series of climaxes like this. That was why there was such shock and surprise in her wide, glistening eyes, which were drowsy with pleasure. That made him feel so powerful, so masculine, and at the same time so protective of her. His heart soared with the knowledge that she was like a virgin in one way—never touched, never loved as she should be loved or explored as a woman.

Knowing that, he leaned down and cherished her parted lips. Little by little, her body lost its tautness after the unexpected climaxes, and he smiled as he drew away from her mouth. She looked deliciously kissed, her mouth soft from his assault, lips wet and provocative. "Come here," he told her darkly, "place your legs across me...."

Paige felt languorous and dizzied by the heat still throbbing between her legs and in her belly. She could barely hear Thane, much less understand what he was asking of her, so powerful was the explosion he had created within her. She'd had no idea that a man touching her like that could arouse such a fierce, wild storm within her. When she rose unsteadily into a sitting position beside him, he guided her so that her thighs straddled his hips She saw the knowing, the sureness in his hooded eyes, and trusted him completely.

"I—I've never done this before...." she murmured as he settled his strong, large hands around her hips.

"You'll like it," Thane assured her huskily. "Trust me, Paige. Just trust me?"

"With my life," she whispered as she placed her hands against his chest. And she did. She always had. A fierce, overwhelming love moved through her as she met and held his glittering eyes. His hands were warm and sure against her hips. In moments, he was lifting her as easily as if he were lifting a child. Paige had no idea what he was doing until he eased her down upon the full length of his hardness. Then she gasped and squeezed her eyes shut. Her fingers dug into his chest.

"Good," Thane cajoled her in a dark voice. "Good...just let me move you, Paige. Let me show you how good it can be...." And as he moved her sweet, wet body across his painfully hard form, it took every last vestige of his remaining control to keep himself in check. She arched her spine. Her head tipped back. Her delicious cascade of ebony hair flowed down her shoulders and back. She was part animal, part human to him in that moment. Her entire form was a strong bow ready to be unleashed. Smiling to himself, he angled her so that her womanly core met the tip of his throbbing hardness.

The instant he slid into her, Paige felt her body stretch to accommodate his size. The pleasure rippled and intensified. She was helpless; she felt like a puppet, her joints weak, her body melting beneath his exquisite assault. Just the slow, rhythmic movements as he eased into her tightened confines served to make her feel untamed and out of control. Her body burned. It screamed. It tightened around him as he entered her. And yet she knew instinctively that loving him was the most beautiful of all things. With each sliding movement, she took him more deeply into her until they were fused in a hot, slick union.

Something else took over within Paige at that moment: her heart exploded with violent love—love for Thane that had been held at bay for all those years. The feeling mixed hotly with the throbbing heat building volcanically within her lower body. She moaned fiercely as he gripped her hips more tightly. Her breath became suspended. She felt him thrusting into her. Deeply. Forever.

Her back bowed, her fingers curled in that exquisite, pleasurable moment. A cry rose in her throat. It was a cry of exultation, of a woman melding completely with her mate in ferocious union. And then he began to thrust harder and move her more quickly against him. It was too much! Her mind dissolved into bright, spinning lights. They were one. Paige loved him fiercely. Something told her to move with him. She fought her own limp surrender, to grip him and push downward with all her might. Instantly, Thane groaned. It was like wonderful music to her heightened senses. She had just discovered how to return the pleasure he was giving her so freely.

Breathing raggedly, Paige found and established an urgent stride with him. The pleasure grew more and more hot, fervid and reckless, until something white-hot exploded violently through her lower body. Crying out, Paige froze, unable to do anything in those melting moments. She felt him grip her hips hard and continue to thrust deeply within her. The molten satisfaction built and throbbed, built and throbbed until she felt that she could stand no more, and intense pleasure moved through her in wave after wave.

Paige collapsed against him. She could not control herself, or her reactions to the violent explosions he'd created and triggered scaldingly within her. Face pressed against his neck, their perspiration mingling, she felt him stiffen and groan. The sound was primal music to her ears. Paige felt it reverberate like a drum from his body into hers. In that moment, she felt his release deep within her. Smiling weakly, she slid her hand up across his arm and shoulder. And then, just as suddenly, Thane relaxed beneath her.

Their ragged breaths mingled. All she could do in those precious moments of spun gold was to press small kisses to the side of his damp neck as they lay in a tangle of slick arms and legs, her hair spread out like an ebony coverlet across the massive span of his chest. The pounding of his heart matched her own. Nostrils flaring, Paige drank in the masculine scent of him, of the mutual fragrance of their loving. Never had she felt like this in her life. As she lay there, she felt his hard length still within her, still claiming her as his woman, and she had never felt more powerful or strong.

As his hands ranged weakly up across her damp back and shoulders, all Paige could do was give him a wobbly smile from where her head was nestled in the crook of his shoulder.

"You were so good...." Thane rasped, his eyes closed, still feeling the after heat of his release. "Like sweet, hot fire. I think I'm in heaven...." He laughed softly as he caressed her head and pressed a kiss to her hair. "I know I am...."

Absorbing his husky words, Paige savored the feelings, the womanliness he'd brought to life within her. Regaining some of her strength, she eased upward, one elbow on the pillow beside his head. With her other hand, she caressed his sweaty features. The love she saw in Thane's eyes as their gazes met was undeniable. Never had Paige expected to see that. Shaken, her mind barely functioning, she wondered if she was seeing things. Gently lifting her fingers and smoothing away the perspiration from his brow, she smiled down at him.

"You have shown me a whole new world, darling. So new…so wonderful. I never knew it existed…."

He heard her soft, halting admission and his heart contracted with sadness. And at the same time, part of Thane soared like an untrammeled eagle at the knowledge that he could teach Paige so much and truly help her connect fully with herself as a woman. "Well," he whispered, "you might be new at this, but I gotta tell you, sweet woman of mine, you were incredible. I've *never* experienced what I shared with you. Ever."

Joy spread through her. "Really?" Her voice was soft and off-key. His words thrilled her.

A lazy grin spread across his strong mouth. "Really!"

Stroking his hands languidly down her back to her hips, Thane purposely moved beneath her. Instantly, he saw pleasure ripple through her. "You're so easy to give to—to share with…."

The low growl in his voice moved through her like a drumroll. She was so attuned to Thane in every possible way that it astounded her. Her whole body had a warm glow radiating from it now, but when he purposely ground his hips into hers and pressed more deeply into her heated core, little ripples of white-hot heat began, like coals being stoked to life. Surprised, she stared down at him. He had such an arrogant, pleased look on his face. Paige acknowledged he was far more experienced in loving than she was.

"You're really enjoying this, aren't you?" she accused with a breathless laugh of joy.

"Every second of it, sweetheart. Every second of it...." And Thane moved provocatively once again to remind her that he could give her more intense pleasure if she desired it.

Moaning, Paige rested her brow against his. "I never knew," she whispered tremulously. "I never knew...."

"What?" Thane murmured, pressing a kiss to her nose. "What didn't you know? That we'd be good together?" He moved his fingers across her firm buttocks and caressed her teasingly.

Moaning, Paige tensed and flattened out against the length of his hard male form. His fingers wreaked such pleasure in her!

"What don't you know?" he whispered in her ear, feeling her slide like a cat against him once more. She was so sensitive, so responsive to his exploration of her. The hot, fluid honey of her body only made him want her all over again.

When he arched against her, Paige could barely think. The golden glow in her lower body was now ratcheting up once again, like a fire being fed and starting to roar. Only this time he was doing it by stroking her languidly with his fingers and then reminding her he was still buried deep within her. The delight of the throbbing, aching feeling was building rapidly.

Paige sighed, closing her eyes and arching into him. "That it could be like this…so wonderful, so sharing…."

The words haunted Thane, reminding him of all she had suffered. Grimly, he held his anger at bay and concentrated on Paige, on giving her all the beauty that a man could give his woman. She had been so deprived, so cheated, that he once again wanted to get his hands on that selfish ex-husband of hers. Pushing all of that aside, Thane drowned in the exquisite beauty of her moonlit face and graceful form as she moved with him once again.

Silently, he promised Paige that he would over and over again see her smile this beautiful, soft smile now crossing her parted lips. His heart burst with such joy that it caught Thane off guard. The possessiveness he felt toward her, the natural protectiveness, roared through him. Never in his life had he felt like this toward any woman. Not ever. He had no time to look at these new feelings that now embraced him, supported him and lifted him into a euphoria where thinking was impossible. All he could do was instinctively share those feelings with the beautiful woman who had captured him with her large, giving heart.

Chapter Ten

Glancing at the dark leather watch on his left wrist as he ran down the sloping mountain trail, Thane felt a surge of power tunnel through him. He was going to make it! He was going to make the time he needed! The strong June sunlight beat down upon him, turning his already tanned upper body even darker. He breathed easily. His legs pumped. Ignoring the constant pain that was there every time he landed on that injured right leg, he felt euphoric. The fifty-pound pack he carried jammed against his lower back with each powerful stride. He was less than a mile away from his goal.

Up ahead, he saw Paige in her jeans and short-sleeved pink blouse standing beneath the wide, spreading arms of a magnificent old Arizona syca-more, its white bark bright even in the shade. His

heart exploded with such feelings for her. Sweat
trickled off his face, held in a tight grimace as he
ran. He felt the rivulets flowing across his naked
chest. The straps of the military pack—exactly the
type he carried on missions—were cutting into his
hardened flesh, but he didn't care. What was important was being able to carry such weight once again.
Running with only a pair of red-and-yellow Marine
Corps shorts on and a good set of running shoes, he
felt the sun embrace him.

His heart lifted even more as he saw Paige leaping
up and down. He heard her shouting, encouraging
him to run faster. The stopwatch in her hand was
held high. The joy on her face was unmistakable. He
pounded down the slope, lengthening his stride. The
trail had been worn down to red clay since he'd
started these five-mile runs back in March. Each day
he got a little stronger. He had gone from a walk to
a trot, and now a full run.

Half a mile from his end point, Thane sprinted.
Pain shot up his right leg. He ignored it. For the last
month he'd been putting unbearable demands on that
leg. He had to, in order to be able to requalify for
his status as a Recon Marine and be mission available once again. Gritting his teeth, Thane pumped
his thick, muscular arms. His lungs were in superb
shape. His breathing was easy, despite the rigors of
the five-mile run.

Paige was shouting in earnest now. "You're going
to make it! You're going to make it!"

Her cry was music to his ears. He kept up the hard,
striding pace. Every day, Paige was out here at
6:00 a.m., stopwatch in hand. Every day she helped

him with the pack straps, made sure his shoelaces were double knotted so they would not come loose during the run and accidentally trip him. And every day his heart bled a little more. Soon he would be leaving her—and this ranch—and his mother. Three things he'd grown close to, for the first time in his life. Before, he'd avoided intimacy like the plague. Maybe it was because he had moved so often throughout his life, until his mother had helped him sink roots here in Arizona. Somehow, these two women, in their own unique ways, had woven themselves into his heart. Thane had allowed it to happen for the first time in his life.

Sweat drifted down into his eyes. He blinked rapidly and surged forward the last quarter mile, pushing his body to the edge.

Though low on the horizon, the sun was already strong and burning. Thane grinned a little at the joy written across Paige's glowing face. How much he needed her! Every day with her was one of unparalleled happiness in his life. Every night she went to bed with him—snuggled against him, held him—and they talked, for hours sometimes. And he absorbed every detail of her body against his—her hand drifting gently across his arm or over his chest, the soft moistness of her breath against his flesh as she slept.

How often had he jerked awake at night in the throes of a flashback from his last mission and she'd awakened, sensed his terror and panic, and taken him into her strong, womanly arms and held him? Simply held him and rocked him and whispered that he was safe. Safe… Emotions rose, strong and choking, as he neared the finish line at the gate leading to the house. He was going to leave Paige. And this house he'd come to value much more than he'd ever thought he would. And his mother, whom he'd grown so close to in the last nine months....

"You did it!" Paige whooped, leaping up and down and yelling victoriously as Thane raced past the gate. Her hair lifted and flowed across her shoulders as she turned and ran to him. Bent over, his hands on his knees as he sucked in deep drafts of air, he glanced up at her as she grinned victoriously at him.

"You did it, Thane! Look at this time." Paige held the stopwatch beneath his nose so he could read it. "What a run! You've beat the time the Marine Corps set for you to requalify. Isn't that wonderful?" The victory was bittersweet for her and she tried to keep the sadness out of her voice. Watching as Thane slowly straightened and then moved his massive shoulders to get rid of the pack, she stood back. This was a morning routine she had come to love. Watching Thane grow strong once again, seeing his magnificent body grow hard from the stress he put it under. Paige had had no idea about the military or what it demanded of its people. She did now.

Handing him a towel she kept on her belt, she met his gleaming eyes. The look in them was for her only. Paige saw desire banked in their green depths. Automatically, her body responded hotly to him. The last six months had been the happiest of her life. Standing there, watching him mop his sweaty face and powerful, darkly haired chest, Paige was glad she'd made the decision to love Thane with everything she possessed. Ultimately, she had always known he would leave her and go back to the Corps. He'd never swerved from that goal, and she had accepted what he'd wanted without ever begging him to reconsider.

Grinning, Thane reached out and curved his hand around her neck, her thick hair tangling in his fingers. Drawing Paige gently forward, he leaned over and kissed her hard and long. Her mouth was soft, sweet-tasting like the cinnamon roll she'd eaten hurriedly before his run. As her hands curved artlessly around the thick column of his sweaty neck, he crushed her slender, giving body against his hard one. Soon she would not be with him. Soon they wouldn't be sharing such kisses. A slight glimmer of hope still lingered in his pumping heart. Maybe—just maybe— he could talk Paige into coming to Camp Reed and living with him. As Thane lifted his mouth from hers, he saw the gold flecks of desire in her half-closed eyes. She made him feel so strong, as if he could do anything.

"I like the reward at the end of the run best of all," Thane told her in a low, growling tone, still breathing hard. Releasing her, he looked at the stop-watch once again. "Not bad, eh?"

Paige stepped away, her lips tingling hotly from his branding kiss. She smiled up at him. "Not bad at all, Captain. I'd say Dr. Briggs is going to be more than a little blown away by the fact you're running five miles a day like this."

"With a fifty-pound pack," he said, sending a dirty look toward the pack, which he'd placed against the black, wrought-iron fence that surrounded the front of the yellow stucco, Santa Fe style house.

"The doctor is going to be impressed. I know he will."

"*I'm* impressed," he exclaimed with a chuckle. Mopping off the worst of the sweat rolling down his shoulders and chest, he looked around. He could see his mother in the distance, riding a bay quarter horse and herding about fifty head of cattle into another pasture to the north of them. How strong and confident she was. He would miss her…and the ranch…and the sounds of nature that surrounded him at night, giving him such deep, healing sleep as he recuperated. Usually, his sleep was restless no matter where he was in the world. Here it was different. Thane had come to realize that because this was home, he somehow knew he was safe, and therefore didn't sleep on guard as he usually did. Glancing over at Paige, he also knew she had a lot to do with the peace he felt here.

"I'm going to grab a shower. Then I'll fix us some mean-looking omelettes," he told her with a wicked glint in his eye. Hefting one strap of the pack over his shoulder, Thane took a step on his right leg. Pain shot upward as it usually did, but it was not enough to stop him. And like all days, Paige would pack his ankle and foot in ice after the harsh run to keep swelling, which always occurred afterward, at a minimum.

She met his smile and opened the wrought-iron gate. "You're on, pardner."

The birds were alive with song this morning. Or maybe it was always so and Thane just hadn't been aware of it before. Of late, his senses seemed so much more alive. As he followed Paige up the wooden steps to the porch, past the handmade rockers, Thane watched her move. She had such natural grace, such a slim, tall body. And how loving she was. Moving into the house with her, he shook his head. Oh, he'd had women before. A number of off-again, on-again relationships, but nothing to compare with what he shared with Paige. Maybe it was her Navajo upbringing that made her the way she was, Thane wasn't sure. She was a wild, earthy woman in his arms and he liked her boldness and the searing passion she shared with him. There was such honesty in her, in her kisses. The trust she had in him was so total that at times it took Thane's breath away. And sometimes, when he held her in his arms after they'd made love, he wondered if the woman he held was some kind of beautiful, sacred animal in human form. She was part of Mother Earth. Part of Father Sky. He enjoyed listening to her talk about how she saw the world. The Navajo were deeply in touch with all the natural rhythms of life, something that he had never been attuned to. She had been teaching him about it more and more each day that they spent together.

As Thane moved to his bedroom, he called out, "I'm going to take a shower first. Meet you in the kitchen?"

Paige halted at their room. "I'll get the eggs and veggies ready for you?"

Thane nodded and winked at her. She looked so damned fetching in her clothes. Not that they were tight or revealing, just the opposite. Her pink blouse was buttoned up to her collarbones and the jeans she wore were loose so that she could move and ride a horse easily in them. Paige never wore any makeup. And she needed none. The high, pink flush in her cheeks and the sparkle in her cinnamon eyes were enough to make him want her in every conceivable way.

"You'd better leave now," Thane growled in warning, "or I'm liable to drag you off into the shower with me, lady. You're looking very good to me right about now...."

Breathless, Paige met and held his burning, narrowed gaze. She absorbed his very male inspection as she watched him climb out of his shorts and stand naked before her. His shoulders were held back with natural pride, his chest wide and darkly haired. Her gaze was appreciative as it slid across his flat, hard stomach, narrow hips and below. A fetching smile played across her lips. Raising one brow, she said in a sultry tone, "You're almost too good to resist, Captain. I think I'll leave or we'll never get to breakfast!"

His deep laughter rolled down the hall as Paige turned and hurried to the bright yellow kitchen. She tried to protect herself from the fact that one day soon, Thane would be gone. How was she going to go on without him? How? Leaning down, she retrieved the big, black iron skillet and placed it on the gas stove. Pushing her thick hair away from her face as she straightened, she went through the motions of getting out the eggs, the spatula, the bright red and green peppers, onions and jack cheese they both loved to have mixed into their omelettes.

Each moment spent with Thane was priceless. And every minute spent in his warm, supporting and lov-

ing presence meant one less minute they had left together. Frowning, Paige pulled gold linen napkins
from the drawer and set them on the crocheted ivory
tablecloth. They hadn't talked of his leaving—yet.
But she sensed it would happen soon. Just yesterday,
a courier service had dropped off his summer uniform, polished shoes, hat, and all his ribbons. Her
heart had contracted with terror as she saw him carefully lay out his uniform across their queen-size bed,
as if it were a newborn infant to be loved and cherished. She'd stood at the doorway and watched as
Thane neatly placed each one of his ribbons above
the left breast pocket of the tan, short-sleeved shirt.
Tears had flooded into her eyes, and she'd swiftly
left before he'd discovered her standing there behind
him. Paige had run out to the barn and cried until
she had no more tears left.

All the signs of Thane leaving were evident now.
He'd received orders to report to Camp Reed within
the month of July, contingent upon Dr. Briggs releasing him to active duty status. The phone calls had
picked up between him and his commanding officer,
Colonel Duke Slade. And he'd already been assigned
to start a new Recon team, Team Bravo, as soon as
he got to the base. Once there, Thane would have to
hand pick four men out of thirty to follow him into
his next dangerous combat mission somewhere in the
world.

Her throat closed. Paige made the coffee automatically, her heart bleeding with grief over the coming
loss of Thane. Soon, she knew, he would tell her
when he was going to leave. Taking in a ragged
breath, she looked out the window. She saw Judy

returning to the barn. Oh, her heart ached for Thane's mother, too. She knew Thane and Judy had healed their differences—at least on the surface. Sometimes Paige would hear them talking in the den about Thane's growing up years. Paige never disturbed them at those moments; she knew Judy needed that serious time with her son, to elaborate and expand upon the ugly family situation that had once existed. Sometimes, after one of those talks, Paige would find Thane out on the front porch, rocking slowly back and forth in a rocker, his face thoughtful, his eyes telling her he wasn't prepared to believe or accept everything Judy had told him about his father.

Paige would sit in another rocker and say nothing. But she'd be there for him because she felt his need of her presence at such times. She saw how he wrestled with his feelings, his tangled emotions so clear in his face at those times that it was hard for her to not get up, go to him, slip her arms around him and give him solace. Sometimes he'd verbalize his thoughts to her, saying that he intended to contact some of his dad's old friends once he got back to Camp Reed in order to learn more about his father's past. Paige would say nothing. She could feel him grappling mightily within himself over the fact that his father, once a god to him, was so very human, and had some terrible flaws. From the way Thane's mouth would purse, the way he would grip the arms of the rocker, his large knuckles whitening, Paige knew he was confused and in pain.

With a sigh, Paige forced herself back to the present, watching Judy dismount from her bay gelding and take the horse over to the water trough for a well-

deserved drink. Paige closed her eyes. When would
Thane tell her he was leaving? She could feel it hanging over her like a guillotine ready to be released
upon her aching heart—and the grief was almost
overwhelming.

It was time. Thane wrestled with his anguish as he
watched Paige approach their bed that evening,
dressed in a pale pink silk gown that brushed her
knees. He sat up in bed and pulled the covers back
for her, gazing at her in the dim light the small lamp
on the bedstand provided. It was almost midnight,
and he was tired, but somehow alert and awake.
Thane knew it was adrenaline making him feel that
way. Fear. He felt fear. Fear of losing Paige... As
she threaded her long, slender fingers through her
recently washed and dried hair, his heart contracted.

Patting the sheet next to him, he murmured,
"Come over here, I need to share some things with
you...."

Paige halted midstride, caught herself and moved
around the side of the bed. It was time. He was going
to tell her he was leaving. Swallowing hard, she
avoided his glittering eyes. As he lay there naked,
the sheet across his hips, he evoked desire in her, yet
the look in his eyes confirmed her worst fears. Trying
to pretend everything was all right, she slipped into
bed and lay down beside him as his arm went around
her.

"Comfy?" he murmured against her damp hair,
which smelled of lilacs—Paige's favorite flower. As
her golden arm moved across his hard belly, he tried
to ignore the fluttering sensation her touch created

within him; he needed to check his desire to simply love her tonight.

"Mmm, yes…" She burrowed her head into the crook between his shoulder and neck. Closing her eyes, her heart pounding wildly in her breast as she lay against his chest, she wondered if he could sense her fear. Her grief. Her emotions began to shred. Somehow, Paige knew she must control them—for his sake.

Moving his fingers across the soft slope of her flushed cheek, he whispered unsteadily, "I think you know what's coming. We've never hidden anything since we started loving one another." He saw her lashes barely lift. Paige would not meet his gaze, but he didn't blame her. His chest was on fire with anguish. The *last* thing he wanted to do was hurt her— yet here he was, doing just that. Of all the people he'd ever met in his life, Paige was the one who deserved nothing but happiness after the hell she'd had to endure.

Clearing his throat, Thane allowed his hand to rest on her shoulder. "Dr. Briggs gave me the okay to go back to work. I called my commander earlier today. They're expecting me to report for duty at Camp Reed two days from now."

Her lashes fluttered downward. A soft intake of breath stuck in her throat.

Thane felt her tense. Heard the soft cry slip from her lips, as her arm tightened around his torso. "Damn…I'm sorry, Paige," he whispered roughly, embracing her tightly. "I didn't mean to hurt you— ever…." And he didn't. Holding her against him, crushing her to him, he buried his face in the thick mane of her hair. "The *last* thing I want to do is hurt you. Please believe me. It's the truth...."

Clinging to him, Paige fought to breathe. Fought to hold on to the exploding emotions that were running wildly through her. The feel of Thane's strong embrace helped, but she knew that she would not have his arms around her much longer. Her hand inched up to his shoulder and she could say nothing for a long, long time. All she could do was clutch him, absorbing the power of his masculine body against her own and feeling her heart breaking and shattering within her breast.

"We knew this day would come," Thane told her in a low, broken tone. "I know we never spoke much about it. And I know why. But we've got to face it now, Paige." He drew in a jerking breath. "God, I just never expected it to be so painful. I *need* you...." He squeezed her tightly in his arm.

Tears leaked from her tightly shut eyes. When Thane released her, Paige knew she had to be brave. Somehow, she had to look at him and face the truth. She loved him. He did not love her. If he loved her, he would stay. It was that simple.

As he lifted her chin, she opened her eyes. She could not stop the tears from trickling down her cheeks. To her surprise, she saw tears glimmering in his own narrowed eyes. She felt suffocated. Trapped. This was only the second time she'd ever seen him cry. Her heart broke a little more. Thane had never once said he loved her. And she knew how many times she'd literally bitten her lower lip to stop from telling him of her love for him. It would do her no good to share her love if he didn't love her. Absolutely none.

Choking back more tears, Paige pressed her cheek against his opened palm. "I—I know you have to go, Thane. I just wish it wasn't so soon...but I know your love of the Marine Corps...." She recalled Thane telling her boot camp stories once. About how the drill sergeant had shouted at each one of them that from now on, the Corps was their mother, father, lover and wife, and that nothing else counted. It came first. Always. Family was second. Marriage was second. That had alarmed her. As a Navajo, family came first, last and always. Family consideration was everything, for nothing else of such primary importance existed in the world of the Navajo. Yet in Thane's world, the Anglo world, the Marine Corps provided him with all the things family could provide. When she'd understood that, the full weight of reality had hit Paige. That was when she'd realized she would always be secondary in Thane's life. Just as his mother was. Paige hoped Judy never heard the story from Thane, for the woman had suffered through enough by being a military wife, until she'd been brave enough to make a break from it and live her life in the way she wanted.

Easing his other hand to her cheek, he rasped, "I don't want to lose you, Paige. It doesn't have to be this way. Don't you see?" He saw surprise flare in her wet eyes. He played his ace and prayed it would work. "I want you *with* me, sweetheart. I have a nice apartment over in Oceanside, near Camp Reed. You could live there with me. We could be happy together. I know we could...." He held his breath as he let the idea settle in her mind.

Paige saw the hope burning in Thane's eyes. Heard the tremble in his deep tone. Stunned by his offer, she sat up. Automatically, her hands pressed against her serrated heart, which bled with grief and loss. "But," she cried out softly, "I am Navajo! I cannot leave my family. You *know* that, Thane. You of all people!" And she sobbed, pressing one hand against her trembling lips. More hot tears fell. His image blurred before her. "My heart—my *soul*—are married to this land I was born on, Thane. You know that! Why do you hurt me with such an offer? I would *die* if I left the land here. I have my family obligations—I must help my sisters keep the ranch going. And all my relations up on the reservation that I help and visit...my grandparents would die from shock if they heard I was moving away from them. I love them too much...too much to do that to any of my family."

Wincing, Thane avoided her startled, dark brown gaze. Her tears shattered him, leaving him no hope. Reaching out, he eased his fingers around her hand as it rested against her heart. "I'm sorry, Paige. I'm a selfish bastard. That's all there is to it. I was just searching for some way to save what we have...build on what we have. I've never been so happy as I have been with you. My world is different now, because of you. I was rattrapping my brain for weeks— months—trying to figure out an angle, a way to get you to come with me." Thane's mouth compressed and he lifted her hand and kissed the back of it. "I know you're Navajo." And he almost said, *And I love you for it*, but savagely clamped down on the words. Thane struggled daily not to express his feelings to Paige. She had never murmured those words to him—and he had no right to say them to her if he could not offer her a life together. But it was a helluva battle to keep the words inside him when he wanted to tell her daily how he felt about her.

Sniffing, Paige reached over him and grabbed several tissues from the box on the bedstand. Sitting back down near him, she wiped her eyes and blew her nose. Gripping the tissue in her fist she risked everything. "Why has it escaped you that you could stay here and not go back to the Marine Corps?"

Her words hung over him. It was a fair question. He wasn't about to say, "because you're a woman, you should follow your man wherever he goes." Paige was his equal. And he saw her as equal to him in every way. She had a say in this relationship just as much as he did. Frowning, he stared down at her hand as he engulfed it in his. "It's a fair question," he admitted hoarsely. "I've thought of it, Paige. I really have."

Her heart leaped with hope. "You have?" Her voice was breathless.

Rolling his eyes, he looked around the darkened room. "Many times. I know my mother needs help here at the ranch. I could certainly help her. And—" he turned and gazed at Paige's suffering face "—I would have you near. A man couldn't ask for more than someone like you, sweetheart...."

The silence engulfed them. Paige held her breath as she searched his masklike face. No matter how much Thane tried to hide his feelings from her, she saw his emotions roiling in his eyes.

Risking it all, Paige moved beyond her fear. "Then," she said huskily, her voice tinged with tears, "why don't you stay? If you really have everything you think a man should have, why are you going away? Why are you throwing 'us' away?"

His heart thudded hard. Painfully. Thane held her blazing gaze. Paige had a right to feel angry, and she was justified in asking him these brutal questions. Turning her hand over and opening her palm, the small calluses across it reminding him how hard she worked, he tried to define his answer.

"Because…life as a marine is the only thing I know, Paige. Ever since I was old enough to recognize my dad was an officer in the Marine Corps, I wanted to be just like him. I grew up loving and worshipping him. I liked the idea of being a hero. Being brave. Saving people." His mouth quirked. "And that's what I'm good at—helping save people's lives. It fuels me, Paige. It makes me feel good about myself. I feel like I'm contributing to the human race, not taking away from it. I'm the good guy. The one with the white hat. There's nothing like the feeling I have after a successful mission."

She watched him wrestle with so many emotions. "Sometimes, Thane, there are what I call 'quiet heroes' that walk among us. Oh, I know they aren't out front like you are, and they don't get medals for it, much less any notoriety or pats on the back from others." Her anger surged upward and her voice became strong and passionate as she clung to his gaze. "Your mother is a heroine in my eyes. She went through a hellish mission with your father. She took the bullets in another form, to protect *you*. Granted, she wasn't jumping out of a plane into a dangerous foreign country, but I can tell you this—she *lived* in enemy territory, protecting you for the first twelve years of your life. *That* is heroism in my eyes, Thane. Real heroism. And your mother suffered silently after you left and blamed her for everything. She never once tried to sully your view of your father.''

Paige threw back her shoulders, as if by broaching this subject finally she was throwing off an invisible load she'd been carrying for a long time. ''My sisters are heroines, too. You know why? They fight daily with their hearts, their souls, to keep that tiny sheep ranch of ours going. Why? Because our parents, bless them, had a dream. They had a dream of owning their own land and ranch off the reservation. They wanted to have something for the family that would carry on for generations to come. They bought it with their skimpy savings. They broke their backs building and working the land. And they knew how hard they'd have to work, Thane. They knew from the outset that they'd never live to see the ranch be all that it could be for our extended family one day. But just knowing it was for the family, for the future, gave them the heart and passion to go out there and work from dawn to dusk.''

Her nostrils quivered. Her voice trembled. ''In my eyes and heart, quiet heroes and heroines are just as important as the kind of hero you are and want to continue to be. I take nothing away from you or your goals. But do not insult me or my family by thinking that I would leave them because you do not value the quiet courage they exhibit every day on the ranch, just as you do as a marine. No...I will stay here. My heart and soul are married to this land where I was born.'' She gestured in the direction the sheep ranch lay. ''Someday, perhaps, you will come to honor what I have said, what is important to me, as much as you honor your own life in the Marine Corps.''

Chapter Eleven

"The days are dragging, aren't they?" Judy said as she entered the kitchen and saw Paige standing at the sink, hands in the soapy water. She was looking out the window.

Drawing in a swift breath, Paige turned, one hand coming out of the water in surprise. "Oh...I didn't hear you coming in, Judy." She felt heat rushing up her neck and into her face.

Judy nodded and placed her dusty Stetson on a wooden peg near the swinging kitchen door. "How long has it been? A month now since Thane left?"

Swallowing, Paige frowned and quickly returned to finishing the morning dishes. "Yes," she murmured, her voice soft with longing.

With a sigh, Judy took down a white mug and filled it with steaming coffee. It was noon and time for her to come in and grab a bite to eat before she rode out to her cow and calf pasture to check on the growing babies. "I'm making a peanut butter sandwich. Want one?" she asked, reaching into a cabinet next to where Paige stood.

"N-no, thanks...." Paige scrubbed the big black iron skillet intently. Memories of the times Thane had used it to make their morning omelettes slammed into her hurting heart. No matter what Paige did to try and ease her loss of him, nothing worked. There were so many little things that reminded her of him. And coming over to Judy's ranch two times a week was a cruel reminder of what they'd shared.

"Have you heard from him?" Judy asked as she slathered crunchy peanut butter across the sourdough bread.

"I got a letter from him last week." Paige glanced over at the table. "I brought it along in case you wanted to read it."

Judy smiled at her. "You're the kindest, most thoughtful person I know, Paige. Why that hardheaded son of mine would trade you for his other 'wife,' the Marine Corps, is beyond me. Thanks...I'd love to read the letter."

Paige nodded but couldn't smile. She finished washing the last of the morning dishes in silence.

Judy pulled out a chair and sat down. She reached for the long, business size envelope and avidly read the letter. "So, he's got his team again," she murmured. "I'm sure he's overjoyed."

"Probably is," Paige said, pulling the drain cover out of the sink and allowing the soapsuds and warm water to be released.

"I wonder," Judy murmured, turning and looking over at Paige, "if he's ever going to figure out that he doesn't need to be a paper cutout of his dad?"

"I don't think so," Paige whispered. Wiping her hands on a nearby towel, she rinsed the morning dishes beneath hot water and sat them in the drainer on the counter to air dry. There weren't many dishes to do. Paige just wasn't hungry anymore. She hadn't been since she'd seen Thane off at the Phoenix International Airport four weeks ago. All she could do was cry and feel, and then cry some more. Losing Thane from her life had shattered her.

"How did you deal with it, Judy? The fact that your husband treated you second to his employer, the Marine Corps?"

Chuckling, Judy bit into the sandwich. After a few minutes, she said, "Listen, when you marry a marine, you marry the Corps, too. They make that amply clear to you from the gitgo that the Corps is number one and you're number two. It's the way it is."

Paige grimaced and took off the green checkered apron, hanging it on a wooden peg next to Judy's hat. "Maybe that's why all the services, including the Corps, are losing so many people nowadays. You've read the newspapers. Their retention rate is sliding faster than they can replace the people who are quitting and going back into civilian life. You'd think they'd get it and see the family of the service person as number one, not number two." With a sigh, Paige decided she had to eat something. She'd skipped breakfast and she couldn't afford to skip lunch. Going to the refrigerator, she opened it and studied the offerings.

Judy laughed outright at her comment. Taking a sip of her coffee, she smiled up at Paige as she brought over a fruit salad she'd made last night. As she sat down to join her, Judy said wryly, "That will be the day when the services put *us* first. They should. Maybe someday they will. But believe me, the Marine Corps will be the *last* to get it. They'll resist the longest. I just read that they're thinking of trying to force those that enlist *not* to marry in their first tour." She shook her head. "Ridiculous. You can't stop biology. But then, the Marine Corps forgets at times that these guys and gals they are recruiting are human beings."

Paige spooned the sweet fruit salad into her mouth. The moments lulled between them. She felt so at home here. And she always loved spending time with Judy, who was, in her eyes, a fount of wisdom. But then, the Navajo people honored their elders and listened to them, unlike the Anglos, who often lived apart from their elders and did not take the time to hear about their hard-earned life experience and accrued wisdom.

"Did you see in his letter?" Paige said, pointing to it on the table between them. "That Thane said they're on standby status for missions now?"

Worry crept into Judy's voice. Her mouth became a momentary slash. "Yes, I saw that."

"I don't know whether I could stand being married to a Recon Marine, anyway. I'd die of worry all the time, wondering where they'd sent him and if he would survive it. I mean…look at Thane's last mission in Bolivia. Four out of five men died on that one.'' She shivered.

''Honey, you'd adjust,'' Judy counseled, finishing off her sandwich. She picked up the mug of coffee. ''You do it or you go crazy with fear and worry.''

''Don't they understand that it's hurting us incredibly?''

Judy gave her a sympathetic look. She reached out and squeezed Paige's slumped shoulder. ''I know you love him, Paige. And that's the hardest part— loving a marine who is about to go into combat.''

There was that word again—*love*. Paige pushed the fruit salad away, her appetite completely gone. As Judy lifted her hand from her shoulder, Paige said, ''I never told him that, Judy. I wanted to, but…''

''But you thought by telling him, it would force him to stay here and not go back to the Corps?''

Nodding, Paige rubbed her hands against her face, trying to get rid of the pain in her heart that never seemed very far away. Every time she thought of Thane, which was almost every waking minute of every day, her heart would twinge as if a sword were being jammed through it and cruelly twisted.

''I thought it over very carefully, Judy. If I'd told Thane I loved him, it would maybe…force him to stay. And I didn't want him to stay because of that. I wanted him to stay because he *wanted* to—for all the right reasons…such as being responsible to you, his mother, and to this ranch. He saw how badly you need help.''

''I know, I know,'' Judy soothed. ''Thane tried his best, Paige. He's sending money to me monthly to help me out. I never expected that of him and it was a wonderful surprise and gift. In his own way, he's telling me he loves me, and that's more than I ever hoped for.''

Frustrated, Paige got up and placed the lid back on the container of fruit salad. Going to the refrigerator, she opened it and set the fruit salad on a shelf. ''That's what most Anglos do nowadays—they throw money at their parents or elders, thinking that it will fix the situation and they'll be free and clear of the responsibility for them.''

Shutting the door, Paige poured herself a cup of coffee and joined Judy back at the table. ''No, I wanted Thane to stay for the right reasons, Judy. And he obviously sees life differently. He doesn't have Indian blood. Lots of Anglos have released the need to be responsible for their elders, for the help they might need as they grow older. It's a society thing, I guess.''

Judy nodded. ''There's nothing anyone can do about it. Thane saw how hard I work around here. And he knew the budget I wrestle with monthly. I'm grateful he came up with the idea, all on his own, to send me some money every month. That *will* help, and I'm grateful to him. Considering where we were with one another when he came home, our relationship is wonderful now.''

Paige nodded and sipped the hot, black coffee. ''I know it is. And I don't mean to make you think that Thane's a bad person, because he isn't. He just doesn't see the world like we do.'' She offered Judy a weak smile. ''I wish he would have chosen to stay here and not go back to the Marine Corps.''

"I think there's more to it than what we see," Judy murmured, finishing off her coffee and rising. She rinsed out the cup and set it in the sink. Her face was thoughtful as she turned and studied Paige. "When he kissed you at the airport, I saw the look in his eyes. It was a look of a man not wanting to leave someone he loves deeply. You."

Again, pain skittered through her heart. Paige closed her eyes. "Yes…I saw it, too. But it didn't make a difference, Judy. I was so hoping—" Her voice broke and tears flooded into her eyes. "Oh…I'm sorry," she murmured, flustered. Rising, she hurried to the kitchen counter and pulled several tissues from the box there. Dabbing her eyes, she tried to control her emotions. "I just can't stop crying, Judy." And she sniffed again.

"Oh, honey." Judy came over and wrapped her long, thin arms around Paige. She hugged her fiercely and whispered, "Thane loves you. I'm hoping that over time, his love for you will outweigh his love of the Corps." Releasing her, Judy gently brushed an errant strand of hair away from Paige's flushed face.

"I know the logic. But my heart doesn't understand it at all," Paige admitted hoarsely. She hastily blotted her reddened eyes and blew her nose.

"Thane has to go back, Paige. He's got to weigh and measure what he *really* wants out of life. He spent six months with you. He found out what love is. When it's good, it's great. And judging from what I saw of the two of you when I was around, your love is solid. There aren't many men who are blind or stupid enough to throw that kind of treasure away."

Paige made a face and sighed. "Well, your ex-husband did. He was blind *and* stupid."

Laughing uproariously, Judy slapped her knee. "You've got a point, Paige. Well, I'm hoping and praying that Thane isn't a chip off that particular block! I'm hoping my genes, my example will influence him to know that home is where the heart is—not chasing some fading dream that his dad created for him. No, Thane has to first deal with what he recently learned about his father's antics. Thane said that at some point when he got back to Camp Reed he was going to talk to his father's cronies—the marines who knew him well. And if those guys will come clean and tell Thane the truth, I think it's going to shake his neatly tied little world."

"And then what will happen?" Paige wondered.

Judy rolled her eyes. "I'm hoping Thane will leave the Corps and come home to us. I'm hoping he'll realize that maybe his father's life doesn't have to be his. That he's a young man with his own individuality and dreams. I don't think Thane has ever dreamed of anything other than walking in his father's shadow."

Sniffing again, Paige took several more tissues from the box. "I just don't understand it all, Judy. If he *really* loved me, how could he leave me? I could never do that to him."

Judy tilted her head and gave her a compassionate look. "Thane asked you to leave here, didn't he? You love him? Yet you couldn't leave your family, the land you were born on."

Paige struggled to understand what she was saying. "Yes?"

"Well..." Judy sighed, opening her hands "...you're each stuck in your own particular reality, from where I stand. Each is saying: 'my world or nothing.' You obviously love one another. That's not the question. The real question is who is going to give in first and go to the other?" She smiled a little. "And only time is going to answer that question, honey."

Comprehending at last, Paige said, "You're so wise, Judy. I didn't see that or understand it. I was confused by Thane leaving. I see now that we both had choices in this. I was blaming him for *his* choice, but not questioning my own."

Grinning, Judy said, "Exactly. It takes two to tango, Paige. Who knows what will happen?"

Paige blew her nose again. She gripped the tissue in her hand. "I can't leave here, Judy. I would die. I know I would. My family is too important to me. My grandparents...well, they're in their seventies now. They need our help, our support." Paige looked out the window at the hot, bright August day. "Monday evening, the three of us—my sisters and I—are going to take the truck up to Flagstaff, to the forest, and start chopping and gathering wood for them for this winter. Without enough wood, they'd freeze to death because they live in a hogan out in the middle of nowhere. There's no electricity. All they have is a wood stove to keep them warm. I guess Thane doesn't realize these things...."

Moving over to her, Judy slid her arm around Paige's shoulders and hugged her gently. "Give him time, honey. Time usually winnows out the wheat from the chaff. I never gave up the belief that someday, Thane would come home and we'd have a chance to talk over the problems that sat between us. And see? It happened. No, we just have to wait. He's a wonderful son, a man with a good heart. He just has to sort out what's really important to him, is all...."

Thane looked out the window of his office. Dusk was settling in. Everyone had gone for the day. It was Friday and men who were married were hurrying home to their wives and children. Him? His thoughts, his heart, automatically turned to Paige. Turning, he gazed at the gold framed photo of her that sat on his gray, metal military desk. He'd taken that photo of her one day when they'd sat beneath the spreading arms of the white barked Arizona sycamore, enjoying an impromptu picnic lunch. She'd surprised him after his run. When Thane had realized she'd made all his favorite foods, and even brought along a chilled bottle of chardonnay wine, his fierce love for her had overflowed.

Being in love was wonderful. And painful. He moved back to the desk and picked up her photo. It was a head shot, showing her hair loose and free about her shoulders. The look in her cinnamon-colored eyes was one of absolute joy, the gold flecks sparkling in them as she gazed up toward him. Her full lips were parted and the breeze had blown several strands of hair forward to frame her oval face. She was excruciatingly beautiful, so wild and natural looking. Setting the photo back down carefully on his desk, which was strewn with papers, Thane scowled.

He was so immersed in his feelings for Paige, in the fact that he knew without a doubt now that he loved her, that he failed to hear footsteps coming down the highly polished tile hall. A sharp rap at his opened door made him jerk his head upward.

"Captain Hamilton?"

Thane saw a general standing expectantly at the door.

"Yes, sir!" He instantly snapped to attention. It was Brigadier General John Holding, one of his father's best friends. Shocked by his sudden appearance, Thane stared as the tall, lean man with a bull-dog face and icy blue eyes crisply entered his office.

"At ease, Son." Holding removed his hat with inborn precision and tucked it beneath his left arm. "I'm sorry I didn't contact you sooner, but I just flew in on a bird, and I'll be on my way in about an hour. You put a call in to me about a month ago saying you had some questions you wanted to ask me about your father?"

Thane quickly came around the desk and shut the door. "Yes, sir. Please, sit down, sir." He drew the gray metal chair over for the general. Heart beating quickly, Thane watched as the lean, silver-haired warrior sat down, his back ramrod straight.

Swallowing his shock over the general's unexpected appearance, Thane stood there in a parade rest position, his hands clasped behind his back, his feet slightly apart.

"Thank you, sir, for coming. I didn't expect it...."

Holding's watery blue eyes crinkled. "How can I help you, Captain?"

"Sir, this is personal. I hope...I hope it's not a

waste of your time, or that you'll take offense at the questions I have.''

Holding stared at him. "Fire away, Son. I was your father's best friend. He might be gone now, but he's not forgotten.''

Thane took a deep breath, knowing he was taking a chance. Holding was a powerful man in the Marine Corps. And if he was offended by the questions Thane asked, Thane could find himself out of the Corps faster than he could blink. The old guard marines took care of their own, and he knew the protectiveness they could employ. He wasn't sure if Holding would be honest. More likely evasive. But Thane had to try. Thus far, four men he'd talked to who had known his father had provided some information, and none of it was positive—but they all sidestepped the key questions, the questions he needed real answers to. Would Holding be honorable and completely honest with him? As Thane perused the man's sun-darkened face, the hard line of his jaw, he wasn't sure.

"Sir, some sordid things have come to my attention through my mother, regarding my father. I...'' He hesitated. "I need corroboration on them, sir—one way or another....''

Holding's eyes flickered. "You need proof, Captain?''

"Yes, sir, I do....''

Holding's mouth thinned. "Very well. What do you want to know?''

His stomach knotted, but Thane forced himself to continue. "My mother, Judy Hamilton, suffered bruises at various times and a broken arm. I was only a kid back then, sir, but I do remember her injuries. At the time, she had told me she'd slipped and fallen.''

Holding's eyes narrowed to slits. ''She did?''

Thane heard the razor sharp edge in Holding's gravelly voice. He knew something. Thane could see it in the general's face, which had softened momentarily. ''Yes, sir…I know that you and my father were based together at that time. I—I was wondering if you could add anything to either of these two incidents….''

Holding let out a long sigh. He stood and scowled.

Instantly, Thane snapped to attention.

''At ease, Son,'' he murmured. Going to the door, he made sure it was shut, and then turned and studied Thane.

''As much as I admired your father, Captain, he had some weaknesses. Bad ones.'' Placing his gold-braided hat on Thane's desk, he leaned back against the desk, his large, scarred hands resting on the surface, and studied Thane in the gathering silence.

Thane watched the man's face, saw the general weighing and balancing what he would say. Thane's heart thundered in his chest. He held his breath, hoping that Holding would tell him the truth.

''This isn't easy,'' Holding warned him in a growl. ''Your mother, Judy, and my wife, Linda, were best of friends. I happened to be home at the time we received a hysterical call from Judy. She said she'd been pushed down the stairs by…your father…and she was asking for our help.'' Holding raised his eyes and nailed Thane with his piercing blue gaze. ''Of course, I went right over to her house, which sat half a block away from ours. I found her in the basement, sobbing and holding her arm. Your father had left. You were still asleep in your room at the time. I called Linda to come over and stay at your house in case you woke up. It was a Saturday morning, so you didn't have school, and Judy always let you sleep in. I took your mother to an emergency room off base, Son. She didn't want to go to the base dispensary for fear that someone might find out what her husband—my best friend—did to her. She didn't want him brought up on charges for what he'd done, because he would have been. Judy knew his career would have been scuttled at that time.''

Thane wiped his mouth. He saw sorrow in the general's face and pain in his eyes. ''Why didn't *you* turn him in, sir?''

Wincing, Holding said, ''Looking back on it, Son, I should have. But Judy convinced me otherwise. I stayed with her in the emergency room while she got her arm taken care of. She begged me to not turn him in…to not harm his career. She swore this would never happen again. I believed her,'' he said heavily.

Anguish soared through Thane. ''And what about other times, General. Were you there, too?''

He nodded hesitantly. ''Yes. Judy called Linda, and she called me at base ops, where I had duty. She told me she needed me to come home. That it was an emergency. She didn't say what *kind* of emergency. I got someone to take over my duties and came home. You were in bed, asleep, the second time. Your father and mother had gotten into a terrible fight and Judy had asked him for a divorce and he'd beaten her up—real bad. He'd hit her in the jaw, cracked it.''

Thane closed his eyes. He came out of the at-ease position. "My God…" he rasped. "She never told me about her jaw being busted up…."

Holding compressed his mouth. His words came out low and hard. "The worst of it was that he turned and headed up the stairs to beat you up in order to get even with your mother. She ran after him. They fought on the stairs. He pushed your mother down them, then and that's when she broke her arm a second time. At that point, your father left the house. You were safe."

Thane stared openmouthed at him.

Holding scowled. "I can guarantee you, Son, that when I found your father, we had words. As much as I admired him, respected him, I couldn't let this go. We had it out at my office, later, after we got Judy to the emergency room. I had her admitted to the civilian hospital for observation. She never told anyone what really happened then, either."

"I remember Linda, your wife, sir, coming over and staying with me that morning when I got ready to go to school. She took me to see my mother after school was out, and said she'd had a bad fall." Thane tried to keep the anger out of his voice. "I remember being upset. She had a black eye and her arm was in a cast…"

"Yes…and your father came back home later that night, too. That was after our 'talk.' I told him that he either had to give your mother a divorce and leave you alone, or I would turn him in and get his butt booted out of the Corps. There's no place in it for men who abuse their wives or children.'' His eyes flashed. "And I came within seconds of putting my fist into his face. I wanted to take revenge on him for what he'd done to your mother. Most of all, Son, you need to know this—your mother was afraid that your father would turn on you again. She was frantic to protect you. Linda and I helped her all we could. We supported her unconditionally during the court proceedings and we helped her pack and move out of the base housing and start your new life in Arizona."

Thane nodded. "I recalled your helping us to make that move." Swallowing hard, he met the general's thawing blue gaze. "Thank you, sir…you've helped me a lot. More than you know…."

Coming over, Holding put his hand on Thane's shoulder. "Your father was a mix of good and bad— like all of us. Only his bad went too far. It's one thing for a man to have his own personal devils, but it's another to take them out on those he loves." He gripped Thane's shoulder briefly and released him. Going over to the desk, he picked up his hat and settled it on his head.

"Any more questions, Son?"

Thane's head spun with the information he'd been given. His heart ached—for his mother. "N-no, sir…you've been a great help. Thank you, sir."

The brigadier general moved to the door and opened it. He turned and sized up Thane. "Your mother was a real heroine, Captain. For what she put up with for so long. For how she protected you from all that was going on in that ugly marriage. She deserves a damn medal. Too bad they don't give them out to women like her. I hope that you can see your father for what he was and wasn't. And that you cherish that mother of yours. Marine wives are tough and strong, and she showed her mettle many times over.''

Thane stood there in the ebbing silence after the general left. Pressing his hand to his wrinkled brow, he reeled from the information. His father...it was true...it was all true. And his mother had still soft-pedaled the truth of it to him. Staggering, he felt his knees weakening as realizations continued to explode through him. Gripping the chair, he sat down before he fell down.

Chapter Twelve

Thane couldn't stop his heart from hammering. He braked the new red Dodge Ram pickup truck he'd bought in California and halted in a cloud of dust beside his mother's home. *His* home now. It was late afternoon. Saturday. Paige would be here. As he eased out of the truck and shut the door, he looked toward the Santa Fe style house. No one was around. Looking toward the corrals and barn area, he saw the red-and-white Herefords, most with calves, in the corrals. His mother was not there.

Where was everyone? He wiped his mouth and moved around the bright red truck toward the wrought-iron gate. The colorfully blooming roses alongside the house were in the shade now, out of the merciless heat of the September sun. He wanted to find Paige. She always worked here on weekends, helping to support his mother any way she could. She was a better daughter to his mother than he had been a son. Well, all that was going to change now.

The gate screamed in protest. Thane added oiling the gate to the mental list of things to do for the ranch as he headed for the screen door and opened it.

"Paige?" he called out. Standing just inside the foyer on a red-gray-and-black woven Navajo rug, he looked around the living room. Everything was just as he remembered it. Swallowing hard, Thane raised his voice.

"Paige?"

The door from the kitchen flew open.

Thane grinned unsteadily as Paige stepped into the room, her hair up in an unruly knot on the top of her head. She had on a white tank top that showed off her beautiful breasts and lean torso and a pair of jeans with dusty knees. In her hand was a dust cloth, and there was a smudge of dirt on her cheek and nose. Her eyes grew huge. Her mouth dropped open. She halted and gasped at the sight of him standing tentatively at the door.

"Thane!"

Her cry, the hope in her voice, shattered through Thane. He heard the anguish, the love in her tone. Paige stood frozen. Probably unsure that he was really there. That he wasn't a figment of her imagination.

He tried to smile, but failed. Holding out his hand to her, his voice cracked as he rasped, "I'm home, Paige. For good. Come here?" And Thane stretched his fingers toward her, hoping that she still loved him enough to come to him. Would she? He wasn't sure any longer. He didn't deserve someone as loyal and loving as Paige, and he knew it. He'd thrown her away in the name of his selfishness. Would she come? Or would she stand there and grow angry with him? Oh, she had a right to be angry, Thane knew.

Paige stared at him. Her heart was pounding. She slowly lowered her arms, clutching the dust cloth in her right hand. Thane looked so unsure as he stood there dressed in civilian clothes. Small gasps of air escaped from her lips as she stared in shock at him. He was so tall, his broad shoulders thrown back with such pride, his face carved by the shadows within the living room as he held his hand out toward her. Paige blinked uncertainly. She had to be imagining this! How many times had she dreamed of him standing there, just like that?

The look on his face was one of hope, and she saw the desire in his narrowed green eyes—for her. Automatically, she responded, that warm, wonderful feeling moving to life within her lower body. Touching her brow, she took a step back. She backed into the door. Partly turning, Paige jerked a look in his direction. He was still there. He wasn't just in her mind, her dreams. He was *real*. Nostrils flaring, Paige looked him up and down. Thane was wearing a long-sleeved white cowboy shirt, the cuffs rolled up neatly to just below his elbows. The blue jeans he wore effectively outlined his powerful lower body and narrow hips. When her gaze fell to his feet, she realized with a start that he was wearing a new pair of plain-looking cowboy boots. As her gaze moved up, she saw that in the fingers of his left hand dangled a light gray Stetson cowboy hat.

Her mouth moved. Her voice wouldn't work. The silence grew thunderous between them. In the distance, Paige heard a rooster crowing. The soft snort of horses. She blinked again.

"You're here...."

Thane nodded. He saw the shock, the disbelief on Paige's wary face. She looked as if she'd seen a ghost. Well, hadn't she? When he left, he hadn't told either her or his mother when or if he'd return home again. What a cruel bastard he'd been. Standing there, he allowed Paige's shock to begin to ebb before he spoke again. All the while, he kept his hand stretched toward her. Would she come to him? Or reject him?

"I should have called, I guess." Thane managed a quirk with one side of his mouth. "I guess I wanted to surprise you and Mother...."

Choking, Paige pressed her back against the swinging door. "What do you mean, Thane? Why are you here? And why are you dressed like that?" Her voice wobbled and tears stung her eyes. Oh, did she dare believe what she saw? He wasn't in uniform. What did that mean? And why had he come here unannounced? Why? The questions clashed in her spinning mind. Her heart was open and wanting him. Wanting him in every possible way, yet Paige was wary. She could not love and lose Thane once more. She simply couldn't stand the daily emotional battering of such a thing again.

"I'm home, Paige. For good. I resigned my commission from the Marine Corps a week ago. I'm coming home to stay." He looked around the quiet house. "My mother needs me...." He grimaced.

Emotions choked him. Then he admitted, "I need *you*, Paige. That's why I came back—for you—and then to be here to help my mother with the ranch." His gaze clung to her widening eyes. He heard her sharp intake of breath. As tears rolled down her cheeks, he began to understand the toll his selfish decision had taken on her. "I—I'm sorry, Paige...for all the pain I caused you. I'm a selfish bastard." He lowered his hand. Paige wasn't going to fly back into his arms. Well, what did he expect after he'd hurt her like he did? He'd thrown their love away. He'd sent her a very clear message that she wasn't of prime importance in his life. The Marine Corps had been, instead. What an utter fool he'd been. Could she find it in her generous heart to forgive him? His mouth was coated with bitterness.

The words slowly sank into Paige's shocked senses. She saw the anguish and hope in Thane's face. As he slowly dropped his arm back to his side and stood there, she saw hope die in his eyes. His proud shoulders slumped. His mouth drew inward in pain. Gulping, she took a step forward, disbelief in her tone.

"You quit your job?"

"That's right. I'm no longer in the Corps."

Blinking rapidly, Paige looked around, then down at the dirty cloth that she was clutching, and up at him again. He was clearly suffering. So was she. "You *quit* your job?"

"Yes. For good, Paige. *This* is my job now. This ranch...."

"Oh no..." And she pressed her fingertips against

her mouth. Tears trailed down between them. His image blurred momentarily.

Thane forced himself forward. He took a couple of steps toward her, the red leather couch between them. He felt the weight of the world crowding in on him. Almost suffocated with anxiety, he whispered, "I know I don't deserve a second chance with you. I understand what I did to you when I left...I was selfish, Paige. I was putting my needs in front of yours. I was valuing the wrong things in life...." Thane stopped, wiped his mouth with the back of his hand and muttered, "I don't know if you can forgive me. If we can start all over. If you'll have me. I love you, Paige. I always did, but I was too damn blind and driven to recognize how important your love was to me—what you gave to me so unselfishly all the time I was here recuperating."

Paige pressed her hand against her wildly beating heart, the dust cloth dangling between her clenched fingers. Closing her eyes, she felt her knees weakening. If not for the door at her back, she was sure she'd have fallen. The words, the sweet words coming from Thane's hard mouth—that same mouth that had worshipped her and loved her and taken her to heights she'd never known existed—were telling her of his love for her. Love. Oh, how often had she dreamed of hearing those exact words? Eyes shut tightly, the tears running down her cheeks, she sobbed. The pain of separation from him exploded through her. All the grief, the sense of loss, overwhelmed her momentarily. Paige lifted her other hand and pressed it over her eyes, ashamed to be seen crying in front of Thane. He would think her weak.

Thane hung his head as he heard her sob. That one sound ripped through him as nothing else ever could. Mouth tightening, he looked away and placed his Stetson on the back of the couch. How much he'd hurt Paige. He was no better than his father in that way, he realized. And there was so much about his father he didn't want to emulate. Thane knew he had some real work ahead of him to separate himself from his father's godlike image.

Savagely, he promised himself he would *never* treat Paige as his father had his mother. Never.

The second sob from Paige made him snap his head up. She was walking toward him. His eyes widened. She was walking toward him, her arms open, her eyes shining with such love for him that it made him groan out loud.

In seconds, she was in his arms, pressing the slender length of her body against his, her strong womanly arms wrapping around his massive shoulders as she nestled her face against the thick column of his neck. Without thinking, he put his arms around her, then crushed her hard against him, his lips finding the soft strands of her ebony hair. When his nostrils flared, the wonderful scent of clean, fresh sage struck him, along with her familiar and wonderful womanly fragrance.

"Paige..." he growled, lifting his hand. He found her face and eased her chin upward. "Look at me, sweetheart...I love you. Do you hear me? I love you."

Her lips, wet from tears, parted as she lifted her

lashes and saw the blazing green light of his eyes as he hungrily gazed down at her. The strength of Thane's body, the support of his arms broke the flood of regret, loss and grief. "Kiss me...." Paige quavered. "Just kiss me. Let me know you're real. That *this* is real."

His smile was very male and very gentle. He caressed her damp cheek and tunneled his fingers into her hair at her temple. "Oh, I'm real, all right." And he leaned down to capture her parted lips.

Never had Thane wanted anything more than this moment. Paige, his life, his hope, was in his arms. She'd come to him! She still loved him even though he'd been a bastard for leaving her! Relief avalanched through Thane as he settled his mouth hotly against hers. She was warm and trembling, and he held her as if she were an adored, priceless jewel. A sob broke from her. He absorbed her pain. Moving his mouth once more against hers, he felt her moan. Her arms tightened around his shoulders and the wantonness of her body pressing against his made him groan with need of her—with the realization that the victory he'd never hoped to have, was now his.

Paige was vibrant and alive within his arms. Her mouth was hungry, eager, giving and taking. His body exploded with heat, with need of her. Just touching her, just inhaling the fragrance of her, sent his senses reeling. He felt her knees giving way as he drank deeply of the offering of her mouth. Staggering slightly, he placed his feet farther apart to keep them both upright. Paige broke their heated, molten kiss and laughed unsurely. He grinned down at her, seeing sun-gold flecks dancing in the depths of her cinnamon-colored eyes. Her tears, he discovered, were tears of joy to be shared between them. His own eyes misted over. Thane tasted the salt of her tears upon his lips.

"I love you, Thane Hamilton...do you hear me?" Paige reached up and pressed her hands to his clean-shaven face. "I've always loved you, but I was afraid to tell you."

The words rang sweetly in his ears. He held her, he stroked her hair, her high-boned cheeks, and he drowned in her tear-filled eyes. "You know what?" he said, his voice low and unsteady. "I don't deserve you. I know that now, Paige. In high school, I was so stupid. I was always drawn to you, but I couldn't overcome my own fear that you might turn me down if I asked you out." He shook his head and held her tightly against him. Her head came to rest against his chest, and he pressed his chin against her ebony hair. Just having Paige wrap her arms around him was all he needed. It told him of her undying love, her long-held hope that he'd return to her. And he had. Finally, he had....

"And I hurt you this time. Badly. I'm sorry, sweetheart. I was so fixated on getting well, getting back to the Corps, that I put you and my mother last in importance in my life. I hope you can forgive me someday. I don't expect it now...but maybe..." Thane closed his eyes, emotions overwhelming him momentarily. His voice cracked. "I hope...over time...you can forgive and forget. I'll work hard to earn your trust again. I'll earn every inch of it, Paige. I swear I will."

His words were like a dream come true to Paige,

but when she felt him tremble, she realized the words coming out his mouth were filled with such pain that she could hardly stand it. Easing away from him, Paige gripped his hand and whispered, "Come, sit down. Talk with me…."

He came like a lost little boy. Paige understood that he trusted her with his life, and that knowledge empowered her and engaged her quiet strength as a woman. As they sat down, their knees touching, their hands wrapped within one another's, she whispered, "Something made you change your mind, darling. What was it?"

Thane closed his eyes and hung his head. Just the steadying, loving touch of Paige's work-worn hands over his gave him the courage to speak. "It's pretty ugly, Paige. I don't know if my mother ever told you about it."

"About what?" She tilted her head and gave him a gentle look. There was such agony in his eyes. The way he worked his mouth, the shame she saw in his gaze, tore at her heart. Tightening her grip on his large, strong hands, she whispered, "You can tell me, Thane. I'll listen."

Taking a deep breath, Thane launched into the story that General Holding had shared with him. Time seemed to freeze as he told Paige everything. Thane could tell that she had not known the depth or details of his mother's escape from his father. Or that Thane had been the next intended target of his father's unreasoning rage and jealousy. When he finished, he gripped her hands tightly. He saw the shock in her face. All the color had drained from her cheeks. Her eyes were dark with disbelief.

"He was coming after *you?*" The words exploded softly from her.

"Yes." Thane looked around and took a deep breath. "My Mother never told you?"

"Gosh, no…" Paige shook her head. "In college we had to take psychology courses. I remember studying personality disorders, and how one type of parent would become jealous of a son or daughter when they reached puberty—twelve or thirteen years of age—and then try to destroy them." Shivering, Paige chewed on her lower lip and stared at Thane. "And your mother stopped him on the stairs…before he reached your bedroom. Oh…" She took a ragged breath. "How awful for Judy! No wonder she took you away and filed for divorce, Thane."

Grimacing, Thane looked around the quiet room. His mouth worked to keep the emotions he felt under control. Just the gentle way Paige was behaving helped him speak of the terrible wound that lay open in him. "After the general left, I sat down in shock. I couldn't…didn't want to believe him. But I knew he was telling the truth. He had no reason to lie. My father was his best friend." With a shake of his head, Thane held her glistening gaze. "I don't know how long I sat there. I remember looking at my watch, and it was past midnight. I'd been rattrapping with my brain, all my memories as a kid growing up…and I do recall times that my father would make fun of me. He'd push me around, but I thought he was doing it for fun, to toughen me up to be a marine someday."

"Was that when you were older?"

"Yeah…I was nine when he started that rough

kind of play with me. I remember...*now*...that my mother would stop it. She'd come in and stand between us. And then my father would get mad and start shouting at her. I'd run, Paige. I'd run to my room and shut the door.'' Sheepishly, Thane looked away and muttered, ''And I'd hide under my bed.''

Her heart broke. ''Oh, darling...'' she reached up and grazed his cheek with her hand ''...there's no need to feel shame about this. You were a young child—your heart was wide-open. You trusted your parents. Especially your father. Of course you ran and hid. When parents start yelling like that, it's enough to scare *any* child of *any* age.''

Nodding, he wiped his mouth with his hand, then took her hand in his again. Thane desperately needed contact with her in every way. ''Why didn't my mother tell me the rest of this, Paige? That's what I can't figure out. Why did she continue to hide it from me? If I'd known about it...well, maybe I wouldn't have left here. Maybe things would have been different.''

Paige shrugged. ''Knowing Judy as I do, I know she has always tried to protect those she loves. I've seen her do it with me.'' And Paige gave him a soft smile. ''After you left, Judy knew how much I was hurting. She was so wonderful with me, so supportive. If it hadn't been for her, I'm not sure I'd have survived it—your leaving, I mean....''

''Damn...'' Thane caught himself. He closed his eyes. ''I'm sorry, Paige. So sorry I caused you that much pain. I'm such a bastard....''

''Hush, darling.'' She pressed her fingertips to the tortured line of his mouth as he hung his head. She met his opening eyes with a tender smile. "My love for you has never died…it didn't since high school. So how could it take flight now? I don't regret what happened. You were growing as a man, a human being…and you made the best decisions based upon where you were then. Now that you know the rest of the story and you understand your mother's actions clearly, you've changed." Paige gave him a proud look as she removed her fingers from his strong mouth.

"Maybe," Thane growled. "I have a lot to atone for. To make up for with my mother…with my past with her."

Paige sighed, raised his hand and kissed the back of it. "You have all the time in the world now, darling. We've always loved you. That is one constant that has never changed and never will. We were hoping you would look at all the evidence and, over time, realize that you did not have to walk in your father's footsteps. That you would come to realize you were unique. You were Thane Hamilton. Not just the son of a Marine Corps general. Judy and I hoped that you would want to explore and find out who you were—not the image of your father, but you, as a human being."

Reaching out, Thane caressed her cheek, which now had color returning to it. "Are women always this wise and us men such fools?"

Laughing, Paige shook her head. "Oh, no! No, you won't hear me say that! Look at me. Look at the mistakes I've made, Thane. I married because I felt I was worthless. I jumped at the first boy who came along who made a fuss over me and made me feel important." Paige grimaced and then opened her hands. "I fell into a trap so many young women fall into, Thane. I had little self-esteem, little belief in myself...and I looked to an immature boy to fill in those missing parts of me. Well—" she rolled her eyes "—that was a big mistake. Johnny didn't have the maturity to do anything, much less be married to me. And when he found out I was pregnant, he couldn't handle the responsibility of being a father and starting a family. Not that what he did was right. Don't get me wrong, I'm not defending him." Paige gave Thane a sad look. "All I'm saying is this—we *all* make a lot of mistakes along the way. I feel what is important is to pick ourselves up from them, learn from them and try to grow because of them and move on to something better and more fulfilling."

Easing his hands behind Paige's head, he released the pin that held her hair up on top of her head. The satisfaction of feeling the strong, silken strands cascade about his fingers made him smile. "You are so beautiful, inside and out, Paige." Placing the silver-and-turquoise barrette on the coffee table in front of them, Thane picked up her hands and looked deeply into her half-closed eyes. Desire was in them. For him.

"I don't deserve you, but I'm going to work hard to earn the privilege of your love and forgiveness."

Whispering his name, Paige leaned forward and placed a tender kiss against the hard line of his mouth. As she eased back, she whispered, "You don't have to do anything, Thane. You're here. That's all that matters. The fact that you've returned says it all. Everything else, over time, will fall into place, darling. Look how well we got along in the six months you and I were here together.''

''It got better with every passing day.''

She nodded thoughtfully. ''Yes, because we worked on it. We loved one another. More importantly, we respected one another.''

''I'll never treat you like my father treated my mother,'' he told her in a low, forced tone. ''I promise on my grave, Paige, I'll *never* lift a hand toward you. That's wrong. We'll talk it out. And if we get angry, and I know we will sometimes, we'll take a time-out, go cool down and then come back to the table and hash the problem out.'' He gripped her hands hard for a moment. ''I swear to you, I'll never hurt you in any way. At least, not on purpose.''

His words brought tears to her eyes once more. Sniffing, she said, ''Thane, you aren't your father. You never were and never will be. Judy took you out of that environment just in time. She protected you from becoming like him. I'm sure you realize that.''

Nodding, Thane said, ''I do now....''

''This is like a dream come true,'' Paige confided, her voice rising with hope. ''I dreamed of you walking through that door and coming home to stay. I told Judy that I'd dream of it almost every night. I thought it was my grief, my loss of you that was making it so.''

''Dreams do come true, sweetheart.'' Thane released her and dug into his pocket for a moment, then grinned a little unsurely as he produced a dark green velvet box and handed it to her.

Paige frowned. ''What's that?''

"Our future—I hope. Look at it, Paige. It's for you...for us...." His world spun to a halt as she carefully took the small box in her hand and looked at it, and then at him. Her eyes widened as she realized what it might be.

"Oh, Thane...is this...?"

Laughing unsteadily, he said, "Open it. See if you like it...." And his heart started beating hard. Would Paige like the rings? Was it too soon to spring them upon her? Was he wishing for too much? he wondered as he watched her gently pry open the small gold latch and lift the lid.

Gasping, Paige saw a plain gold band and a solitaire diamond set in gold filigree beside it. The two rings looked very old. Jerking her gaze to his, her lips parting, she could only stare into his hope-filled eyes.

"D-do you like them?" he managed to croak.

Touching them with trembling fingers, Paige whispered in a choked tone, "Like them? I love them. They're beautiful! They look so old...."

Clearing his throat, he took the box from her fingers and lifted the engagement ring from it. "Before I left for Annapolis at age eighteen, my mother gave me these to take with me. It was the only thing she gave me. This is the wedding set from my grandmother. I remember Mom coming into my room when I was packing. She asked me to sit down for a moment, that she had something to give me. At the time, I was pretty abrupt with her. Normally, we only talked to one another when we had to.

"I was just glad to be escaping this house and running to the military academy. I sat down, but I was restless and in a hurry. She handed me this box and told me that these were her mother's rings. She herself had worn them up until the time she divorced my father, and then put them away. She told me she wanted me to have them and to give them to the woman I fell in love with. I remember that when she gave them to me she had tears in her eyes. Most of all, I remember her telling me she hoped I'd find a woman who would make me happy.''

Paige sighed. "Your mother is something else, Thane. How generous of her.''

"How loving,'' he added hoarsely. "I was such a selfish bastard at the time. I threw the box into my opened suitcase and asked her if there was anything else she wanted.''

"Ouch…''

"Yeah. Like I said, I was a selfish bastard.'' Sighing, Thane held up the engagement ring. "And I'll make it up to her. Right now, I want you to know I've found the woman who has my heart. I know it may be too soon, Paige, but I wanted to let you know I was serious about you. About us…''

The ring blurred before her eyes, the solitaire glinting like sunlight between them. Paige saw it as a symbol of much more than their love. She recognized it as fulfillment of Judy's lost love. Lifting her left hand, she whispered, "Put it on me?''

Stunned that she'd accept, Thane wasted no time in sliding the ring on her slender finger. It fit perfectly, as if it had been made for Paige. "I want to marry you,'' he told her seriously, holding her shimmering gaze as he held her hand in his. "Whenever

you want. You just say the words, and I'll be there.
I'm not going to be so stupid as to lose you again.''

Giving him a tremulous laugh, Paige threw her
arms around his shoulders. "You're *never* going to
get rid of me, Thane Hamilton. Not ever!''

He hugged her hard, until the breath rushed out of
her lungs. How much he loved her! The joy shining
in her eyes as he pulled her into his lap bubbled
through him. "I don't deserve you," Thane murmured roughly, "but I'm going to work hard to do
just that.''

Paige smiled through her tears. Out front, she
heard another pickup truck come to a stop. Lifting
her head slightly, she murmured, "That's your
mother. She's coming back from taking a load of
cattle down to the Phoenix stockyards. I know she's
going to be thrilled you're home—for good.''

Giving Paige a swift, hot kiss on her smiling
mouth, Thane eased them to their feet. He kept his
arm around her waist as he heard the rusty old truck
door on his mother's aged vehicle slam shut. In a
few moments, his mother—the woman who had
loved him and protected him so fiercely—would
come through that door. And her life would change.
For the better.

Glancing down at Paige, who leaned against him,
her arms solidly around his waist as she looked up
at him with such warmth and pride, his heart burst.
Thane didn't deserve her, but he would earn her love.
And he knew that with his mother's wise counsel and
support, his life here at the ranch would be better
than any life he'd ever had before.

"I love you," he whispered fiercely to Paige,
"forever....''

Epilogue

"Well?" Thane asked Paige, "what do you think? Will you be happy in our new house?"

They stood in front of a recently built, Santa Fe style structure. It was several hundred yards from Judy's home on the ranch. The warmth of the early evening June breeze wafted strands of Paige's hair as she stood with Thane, his arm around her waist. She saw Judy coming toward them, a cake in hand and a big smile on her features.

Smiling up at him, Paige whispered, "I would be happy with you anywhere on this land, Thane."

Leaning down, he kissed her smiling lips. Since returning home in the fall of last year, he had wanted to have a house built near his mother's. That way they could be close, but have separate residences. It had taken six months to get the house built, and they had all worked on it, along with the contractor who had been hired to erect the structure. "It's been a real labor of love," he said against her lips. He felt her smile beneath his mouth.

"Yes, well, emphasis on the word *labor,* Mr. Hamilton." As Thane raised his head, Paige drowned in the green warmth of his eyes. They had married in March, and two months later, Paige had found herself pregnant, much to the joy of Thane and Judy, as well as Paige's whole Navajo family.

Chuckling, Thane moved his hand gently across her abdomen. Silently, he swore that Paige would have a safe pregnancy. He hoped that this child would dull the loss of her first baby, the one she'd miscarried. "Well, Mrs. Hamilton, I think Grandma is coming to walk us across the threshold of our new home." He saw Judy approaching, the light in her eyes one of unabashed happiness. She'd slaved all morning making them a triple-layer chocolate cake with white frosting for the celebratory occasion.

Paige turned with Thane and they smiled as Judy came to a halt. Her face was flushed, her grin widening as she held the cake out toward them.

"Well, kids, are you ready to move into your beautiful new home? Can I walk you across? We'll cut the cake in your new kitchen."

Laughing, Thane drew his mother beneath his other arm, and he steered the two women in his life toward the red tile walk that led up to their home. "You bet you can, Mom."

Paige thrilled at the way Thane had healed his wounds with his mother. The past months had been rocky at times, but Paige had watched as they'd worked to heal, and finally, to enjoy one another, on a completely new level. Now they were friends, not just mother and son.

As she stepped gingerly up the brick steps, which Thane had laid himself, Paige sighed happily. Soon her family, all of them from the reservation as well as the sheep ranch, would be arriving for a huge celebration. Her grandmother, a medicine woman, would bless the house in Navajo ways. And she would bless her and Thane, as well as the baby that grew lovingly within her. Sliding her hand across her abdomen, she smiled. In her wildest dreams, Paige had never imagined her life would turn out this wonderful.

Thane released the women and, with a knightly bow, opened the screen door and gestured for them to walk through.

"My ladies? Paige, step across. Mom?"

Paige glanced at Judy. She grinned. "It's almost a carbon copy of your house, Mom."

"It's a good design," Judy agreed, smiling at her.

Paige stepped into the living room, the reddish-colored cedar floor waxed to perfection by Thane. Judy stepped inside next and Thane followed. They all stood there looking into the living room, which had been recently furnished with a leather couch and several overstuffed chairs. Paige cherished the fact that her aunt had made a special Navajo rug for the living room. It was brightly colored in tones of deep blue, lavender and cream, and went with the leather couch and attending wing chairs. Her other aunts were quilters, and they'd worked hard to create a huge quilt with Navajo designs on it for their king-size bed as well as one for the crib and the baby to come. Yes, this house was a family project of the most wonderful kind. On weekends, many of her male relatives had driven down from the reservation and helped Thane work on the roof, do the painting or erect the white picket fence surrounding it. This was a home built by two families. Out of love. And with joy.

Judy sighed and said, "Children, this house mirrors both of you so much. I love the rug—it sets off the red flagstone fireplace and the brass around it." She moved to the kitchen to prepare for the ceremonial cake cutting.

Thane eased his arm around Paige's shoulders and drew her close to him. He always looked forward to having her arm slide around his waist. His life had taken such a remarkable turn, and having Paige to share it with was a miracle for him.

"Well?" she whispered, looking up into his shadowed, thoughtful features, "are you sorry?"

Thane frowned momentarily. "Sorry? For what?"

Her lips curved. "Standing here, in your house, with your wife and your baby-to-come, are you sorry you left the Marine Corps for all of this? Us?"

Thane saw the tenderness in Paige's sparkling eyes and allowed her soft voice to riffle through his heart. He loved her voice, the way she talked, how she framed what she thought into words to share with him. Squeezing her a little, he said, "No, I haven't looked back, Paige. I don't need to...." And he didn't. "In fact—" Thane turned and rested his arms gently across her shoulders and looked down at her fondly "—from where I stand, I'm a man who has more than he ever deserved. Looking back on my other life, I can see now as never before that I was trying to fill my father's boots and be as good as, if not better than, he was. I was chasing a ghost...."

Lifting her hand, Paige brushed several strands of dark hair from his furrowed brow. Thane had allowed his hair to grow a little longer since leaving the Corps, but not too long. "Sometimes I see you thinking, though, darling. At odd moments, I'll see you staring off into the distance, and I know you're thinking of your other life...."

Thane heard the worry in her voice. They hadn't spoken often of him leaving the Corps, and he understood Paige's worry. Catching her hand as she smoothed the strands from his brow, he opened her palm and placed a slow, lingering kiss upon it. Instantly, her cinnamon eyes grew dark and languorous...with desire for him. She made him feel so strong and good about himself. Being wanted by Paige, he'd discovered, was the greatest gift of all in his new life.

"Sure," Thane murmured, releasing her hand, "I think about the Corps sometimes. Mostly about my friends. How they are, if they're doing okay, if they're safe—things like that."

Paige knew that Thane had made a concerted effort to keep in touch with a number of his marine friends. He would sometimes call them, and most often, he would get on the computer and e-mail them. She enjoyed listening to him on the phone in Judy's den, talking and swapping old war stories with his buddies. And from time to time, his military friends dropped by for a visit. Paige had seen the eagerness in Thane's face, the animation that came to his expression when his friends were around. She worried that he had made the wrong decision by leaving the Corps. Was he really happy here? With her? The ranch? His mother? Those things always nibbled at her in moments of unsureness. Most of these worries had come when she'd gotten pregnant, and her doctor, a woman, had told her there were some ups and downs she would experience emotionally. Paige hoped it was only that. As she searched Thane's pensive features, she absorbed the look of adoration in his eyes that was meant for her alone. He was so easy to love. So easy to share with.

"I think I see a speck of worry in your eyes," he teased. "You think I'm not happy here? That I wish I was back in the Corps?" Thane framed her face so she couldn't dodge his gaze as he attempted to read the feelings she was trying to keep from him.

Managing a grimace, Paige rested her hands on his thick forearms. "You're too good at reading my mind, darling...."

"Mmm, so you are worried that I'm going to throw all of this away." He looked around and then down at her, his eyes dancing. "And throw you and the baby away, relegate you to second place in my life so I can *semper fi* one more time?"

Paige watched a catlike smile crawl across his wide, well-shaped mouth. Deviltry was lurking in his eyes. She eased out of his capturing grip. Wrapping her arms around herself, she took a step back from his powerful presence. "Now you're making fun of me, of my worries...."

With a laugh that rolled around the room, Thane

said, "Sweetheart, I'd be insane to give you and the baby away." He swept his hand in an encompassing gesture. "And this house, too. I'm happy here, Paige." Looking critically at her belly beneath the white blouse she wore, he murmured, "I think your fears are surfacing, like the doc said. Hormonal changes are making you a worrywart." Reaching out, Thane touched her flushed cheek. "Hey, I'm not going anywhere. Yes, I like to talk to my Corps friends. And I like them visiting. But as for going back? No, Paige, not in a hundred years."

She nodded and compressed her lips, avoiding his sharpened gaze. "I—just worry, that's all...."

"Like any mother-to-be," Thane whispered, and gently pulled her into his arms and rocked her a little. He felt her melt against him, and groaned over the trust Paige effortlessly shared with him.

"And you like the ranching? You aren't unhappy about all the hard work?"

Clucking his tongue, he chuckled. "What is this? A laundry list we need to go down and check off? Yes, I love the ranch. And I thrive on hard work. You know that better than most."

Paige felt his thick calluses, the roughness of the daily work evident as he moved his hands down her arms and eased her away from him. There was a teasing sparkle in his eyes, but Paige knew he wasn't making fun of her. If anything, Thane was completely involved in her pregnancy. They had already started taking Lamaze classes, and he was fascinated with her pregnancy in all its aspects. She couldn't want a better, more sensitive or understanding partner than Thane.

He saw her lips part. Holding up his hand, Thane said, "Uh-uh…let's clear the air on the rest of the list, okay?" He held up his first finger. "Yes, I'm happy with you. Next, I don't wish to go back to the Corps. Yes, I miss it, but what I miss is the friendship of the men, not the Corps itself. No, I won't go back—ever. Yes, I'm satisfied that I've given myself to my country, and that's done. No, I'm not going to take Morgan Trayhern up on his offer to work part-time for him. Yes, I intend to stay home, twenty-four hours a day, seven days a week, and keep this ranch running. And yes, I'm looking forward to being a father. Yes, I'm scared to death, Paige, but I have you and Mom to help me get over that." And he grinned wickedly. "Let's see—have I left anything off that little worry list inside that beautiful noggin of yours?"

Paige smiled a little, embarrassed that he'd read her like a book. "You *have* been reading my mind, Thane."

Chuckling, he said, "Honey, when you love someone like I love you, it's easy. Very easy."

"Children?" Judy called.

"Oh, Mom's got the cake ready," Paige said.

"Whoa…."

Paige stopped and felt herself being gently turned around to face Thane. He was gazing at her with that particular look that always melted her heart and made her so happy. She laughed breathlessly as she met and held his gleaming green eyes.

"Okay, okay…I give! You went down the whole list and now I'm convinced. Okay?"

Thane studied her, his hands holding hers. Since

she had become pregnant, there was such an ethereal and glorious quality to Paige's face. She had softened even more, if that was possible, and he absorbed her nurturing energy with newfound pleasure. "So, no more worry about these things, right? I'm a happy man, Paige. I'm the luckiest man in the world." He grinned wickedly. "And I *know* it."

Paige's laughter filled the living room. "Oh!" she cried as she threw her arms around his broad, thick shoulders, "I love you *so* much, Thane...." And she did.

As Thane gripped her and lifted her off her feet, slowly twirling her around, Paige clung to him, her arms tight around him, her face pressed against his. Their laughter mingled. It flowed around the room and filled it—the music of life. Of a love fulfilled. Of a dream come true—for all of them. Forever.

*　*　*　*　*

Chapter One

Jake heard faint footsteps on the stairs. It had to be Lieutenant Cortina. A hundred questions whirled through his fatigued mind. Would she be one of those strong, competitive-type women who were in the Army nowadays? Probably.

He saw a woman, her hair black, slightly wavy and falling around her shoulders, peek above the second floor landing. She was darkly tanned, her coloring shouting of her Peruvian heritage. Jake sucked in a breath as she turned her head and continued up the stairs toward him, her slender hand on the rail. As she turned, her cinnamon-colored eyes settled questioningly upon his. Her lips were slightly parted in anticipation.

She was beautiful.

Without thinking, Jake rose to his feet. It was part

of his officer's training to stand in the presence of women, despite his feeling that no woman was up to the job that lay ahead of him. Countering his irritation over Morgan's decision to partner him with Lieutenant Cortina, he moved around the table and pulled out the chair next to his as she hesitated at the top of the stairs, looking at him.

She was dressed in dark green canvas shorts, a red T-shirt that said "Machu Picchu" on it, and well-worn hiking boots. Her cheeks were flushed and gave her wide, intelligent eyes more emphasis.

Jake's gaze moved to her mouth. How beautiful it was—a mouth made for sin. Her lips were full, the lower one slightly pouty and provocative looking. She wore absolutely no makeup, but she didn't need it, in Jake's opinion.

"Are you…" he began awkwardly, holding out his hand toward her. Somehow, he wished she wasn't his team partner. She was too beautiful, too feminine looking to be qualified for such a risky venture.

Ana smiled shyly as she stood uncertainly, her hand resting tentatively on the huge, curved banister. "Jake Travers?" She saw him scowl, his gaze assessing her as if she were stripped naked before him. It wasn't a sexual thing, though. Ana could feel his unhappiness toward her. Like most men, he probably thought a woman couldn't do a "man's job." Girding herself, she tried to coolly return his arrogant gaze.

Jake felt his skin tighten at the sound of his name on her lips. It had rolled off her lips like a lover's caress. Her voice was soft, like a cat's tongue licking him sinuously. Hell, he felt his lower body grow hot.

He managed a curt nod. "Yeah, I'm Jake Travers. You Ana Cortina?" He sounded as snarly as he felt.

She smiled and allowed his glare to glance off her. "Yes," she replied, and moved forward, shrugging the knapsack off from her shoulders. How different Jake looked in person! Ana felt her heart skipping beats, and she felt unreasonably elated at seeing him even though he obviously didn't want her presence on this mission. He was dressed in tan chinos, hiking boots and a black polo shirt that emphasized his tightly muscled arms and broad set of shoulders. His hair was dark brown and cut military short. His face was square with a stubborn, pronounced chin. His lower lip was fuller than his upper one. Most of all, she liked his thick dark brown brows that lay straight across his glacial blue eyes.

"Well," she asked lightly, "do I meet with your approval?"

Taken aback by her bluntness, Jake scowled. It was as if she had read his mind! Shaken, he muttered, "That remains to be seen...."

You're not going to believe this offer!

In October and November 2000, buy any two Harlequin or Silhouette books and save $10.00 off future purchases, or buy any three and save $20.00 off future purchases!

Just fill out this form and attach 2 proofs of purchase (cash register receipts) from October and November 2000 books and Harlequin will send you a coupon booklet worth a total savings of $10.00 off future purchases of Harlequin and Silhouette books in 2001. Send us 3 proofs of purchase and we will send you a coupon booklet worth a total savings of $20.00 off future purchases.

Saving money has never been this easy.

I accept your offer! Please send me a coupon booklet:

Name: _____

Address: _____ City: _____

State/Prov.: _____ Zip/Postal Code: _____

Optional Survey!

In a typical month, how many Harlequin or Silhouette books would you buy new at retail stores?

☐ Less than 1   ☐ 1   ☐ 2   ☐ 3 to 4   ☐ 5+

Which of the following statements best describes how you buy Harlequin or Silhouette books? Choose one answer only that best describes you.

☐ I am a regular buyer and reader
☐ I am a regular reader but buy only occasionally
☐ I only buy and read for specific times of the year, e.g. vacations
☐ I subscribe through Reader Service but also buy at retail stores
☐ I mainly borrow and buy only occasionally
☐ I am an occasional buyer and reader

Which of the following statements best describes how you choose the Harlequin and Silhouette series books you buy new at retail stores? By "series," we mean books within a particular line, such as *Harlequin PRESENTS* or *Silhouette SPECIAL EDITION*. Choose one answer only that best describes you.

☐ I only buy books from my favorite series
☐ I generally buy books from my favorite series but also buy books from other series on occasion
☐ I buy some books from my favorite series but also buy from many other series regularly
☐ I buy all types of books depending on my mood and what I find interesting and have no favorite series

Please send this form, along with your cash register receipts as proofs of purchase, to:
In the U.S.: Harlequin Books, P.O. Box 9057, Buffalo, NY 14269
In Canada: Harlequin Books, P.O. Box 622, Fort Erie, Ontario L2A 5X3

(Allow 4-6 weeks for delivery) Offer expires December 31, 2000.   PHQ4002

Silhouette® —

where love comes alive—online...

#1 *New York Times* bestselling author

NORA ROBERTS

introduces the loyal and loving, tempestuous and
tantalizing Stanislaski family.

Coming in November 2000:

The Stanislaski Brothers

Mikhail and Alex

Their immigrant roots and warm, supportive home had
made Mikhail and Alex Stanislaski both strong and
passionate. And their charm makes them irresistible....

In February 2001, watch for
THE STANISLASKI SISTERS: *Natasha and Rachel*

And a brand-new Stanislaski story from Silhouette Special Edition,
CONSIDERING KATE

Available at your favorite retail outlet.

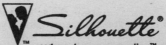

Silhouette®
TM
Where love comes alive™